THE OBJECT OF HIS
Obsession

KIANNA ALEXANDER

The Object of His Obsession

Please note that this book was originally published in 2009 under the title <u>Skye's the Limit</u>.

<u>The Object of His Obsession</u>
by Kianna Alexander

The Object of His Obsession

DEDICATION:

For Tonya, whose "gentle prodding" forced me to finish the first draft of this work, and in loving memory of Brian Keith "Squirrel" Bittle (1968-2003) and Verdis Stone (1922-1999), two men who shaped my life with love and laughter.

The Object of His Obsession

Acclaim for The Object of His Obsession
(*Reviews given during the book's first release*)

"This book kept my interest until the very satisfying end, bringing to a conclusion the problems depicted for every one of the couples and, of course the correct ending for the one creating the havoc. I would definitely read another book by this author. "

-Jaye Leyel, The Romance Studio
www.TheRomanceStudio.com
Rated "Four Hearts"

"...This book has everything, everlasting romance, suspense, best friends and truly wicked family members, as well as, redemption even for a few characters who may not really deserve it...A truly great read, and one I'm more than happy to recommend."

-Regina, Reviewer for Coffee Time Romance& More
www.CoffeeTimeRomance.com
Rated "Four Cups"

THE OBJECT OF HIS OBSESSION

THE OBJECT OF HIS
Obsession

The Object of His Obsession

Chapter 1
September 2004

Skye Lynne Holdron marched purposefully into Fitzpatrick Consulting in West Palm Beach, Florida. Beneath the sensible gray business suit and professional façade lay a very nervous woman. The small, dark scar across her nose itched uncontrollably, as it sometimes did when she stepped out of her comfort zone. She could feel the heat rising to her face as she walked up the stairs toward the second floor office of her boss, David Fitzpatrick.

Outside his office door, she paused, taking a moment to calm her frazzled nerves. She knew what she was about to do was out of character, but totally necessary.

Her dream of owning an interior design firm would be stifled no longer. She had the credentials; her associate's degree in Interior Design was collecting dust on a closet shelf for two years now. Taking a deep breath, she strode in, looking more confident than she felt.

The crotchety, overbearing sixty-two year old was hunched over his mahogany desk, beads of perspiration clinging to his bald head. His large frame overpowered his surroundings; he resembled an angry grizzly bear in a cramped cage.

"Mr. Fitzpatrick," she began.

"Ah, yes, Mrs. Holdron, I've been waiting for you. You're late. I need you to add all of Missy Caruthers's accounts to yours. She's on maternity leave."

She knew he held contempt for the entire concept of maternity leave, and his tone betrayed that fact. Damn him, I can never get a word in edgewise with this blowhard."Mr. Fitzpatrick, I really think you should hire a temp..."

"Nonsense," Fitzpatrick huffed, cutting Skye off again. Frustration crept into his face. "Why pay someone else when I have someone as competent as you?"

He tried to sweet talk her, just like he had in the past. This time it wasn't going to work. "That's flattering, Mr. Fitzpatrick, but as of today, you don't. I'm resigning from my position." Skye watched her boss intently, waiting for a reaction.

Mr. Fitzpatrick frowned, his bushy eyebrows almost touching. "What do you mean, Mrs. Holdron?"

"Well, you ask too much of me. I work many late nights while you and the others go home. I barely have time for myself, let alone my husband. On top of that, you refuse to give me the recognition and compensation we both know I'm due." She leaned over his desk, her face level with his. "I'm sorry, Mr. Fitzpatrick I'm not going to accept this kind of treatment."

"Well, Skye, I assure if you leave Fitzpatrick Consulting, you will not be allowed to come back." His frown deepened to a scowl. "I could care less about your mood swings and your female ranting. You work for me, don't forget it."

"Not anymore, David. Have a nice day." Skye turned to leave, then stopped at the door of his office. "By the way, a little Ex-Lax would probably improve your outlook."

Skye had no interest in hanging around for the fireworks that would follow. As soon as the words left her mouth, she made her escape, moving as quickly as her pumps would allow, out of the building and back to her car.

That night Skye soaked in a bathtub at the home she

shared with her husband, Lawrence. As she lay in the bubbles, her wavy coffee colored hair spilled slightly over the side of the whirlpool, and she smiled.

I'm free. Fitzpatrick doesn't own me anymore. Now I can open the interior design firm I've always dreamed of owning.

For a moment, Skye wondered why she had pursued an MBA and the lackluster ways of Corporate America. Then she remembered -- it had been her dad's idea. But now she was pursuing her passion. No more endless hours of slaving over a keyboard and a stack of paperwork, sipping stale coffee to stay awake. It was definitely time for a change.

The sound of the front door unlocking downstairs broke into her reverie. Lawrence is home. I can't wait to tell him!

Skye jumped out of the tub and stood naked in the doorway to the master bedroom, water and suds running down her body. When Lawrence walked in, a wicked smile graced his lips.

"So, did you..." he began.

"YES!" Skye exclaimed, as she ran into his strong arms. "I quit. I've never felt so liberated in my life." She knew he wouldn't mind her getting his expensive business suit wet. She was naked after all.

As Skye held onto her husband, her eyes lingered on his handsome features. Lawrence was an incredibly attractive, mahogany Adonis. His six foot, two inch frame was like a brick wall. Eight years in the Army left him well-muscled. Staring into his brown eyes, with their unique and unusual depth, always took her back to the day she met him. Those captivating eyes called to her, like an oasis called to a thirsty woman, and she was unable to resist. After ten years of marriage, Skye never looked on another man with the desire Lawrence still ignited in her.

She knew they had something rare and beautiful; there was nothing cliché or rehearsed about their feelings toward each other. Skye loved her husband, quite simply, and she relished the closeness they shared.

"Meanwhile," Skye said, as she pulled away and walked into the bathroom for a towel, "who's going to tell my dad?"

"Not me." Lawrence's face displayed a fake pout as he sat down on the blue plush chaise lounge next to their bed and loosened his tie. "Maybe your parents won't notice."

Skye rolled her eyes as she plopped down at her oak vanity, wrapped in a lavender bath sheet. She dragged a silver plated hairbrush through her damp locks.

"I wish. But you know it was Dad's brilliant idea I get the MBA in the first place. He's always asking about my work. Eventually, I'll have to tell him I quit."

Lawrence removed his shirt. "I sure don't want to tell him. I could do without that stress. I've got two big cases going. But I'll be here for moral support, baby." He rose from the chaise and stood behind her vanity stool, draping his arms over her naked shoulders.

"Why is it the people you love can't just accept your decisions?" Skye looked up into her husband's eyes for the answer to her conundrum.

"I'll always support you one hundred percent."

"But what about..." Skye eyed the growing pile of Lawrence's clothes on the floor near the bed.

"Shhh." Lawrence placed a finger to her lips. "Don't worry about it. At least not now. I want to celebrate your new-found liberation."

"Hmmm," Skye mused. "What kind of a celebration do you have in mind?" She looked at his reflection in the mirror, trying to read his expression.

"The best kind." Lawrence pulled Skye into his arms. "The kind where I turn you out, baby."

Skye shook her head. "After ten years, husband, you're still horny as a toad. I'll bite," she paused, pointing to the floor, "but not until you pick up those damn clothes."

A rueful looking Lawrence obliged her, tossing his clothes into the white wicker hamper in the walk-in closet. Satisfied, she held her arms out to her lovable, but maddeningly messy, knight in shining boxers.

*

Outside, a young man watched the house intently from a sedan parked across the street. He had triple checked the address with his contact, and he knew he had the right house.

1919 West Camino Real. Nice lawn, a Ford pickup and an SUV in the driveway.

The sleepy little suburban Boca Raton neighborhood was full of old folks, so most of the houses on the street were dark, their occupants in bed for the night. He trained his binoculars on the bedroom window, gazing at the silhouette of two people inside the house.

That must be them.

He could see two figures embracing behind the closed Venetian blinds. The lamplight melded their shadows together, until one of them turned the lights off.

Damn. That's all I'm going to see for tonight.

There wouldn't be a lot to report, but it would have to do. Irritated, the man turned away from the now darkened window. He tossed his binoculars into the empty passenger seat, started the car, and left the neighborhood as quietly as he'd come.

*

The next day, Skye was at her bank. She emptied her savings account, and cashed in more than a few of her stocks to realize the dream of opening an interior design firm. She and her best friend, Cammie Hamlin, agreed to be business partners, so they set out on a campaign to get the word out about their fledgling business.

Skye was one of the few people outside Cammie's family who knew her name was Camilla Louise. Cammie, as she liked to be called, was a voluptuous woman of thirty-six. Cammie was her best friend since college.

*

The following day was a sunny mid spring Saturday. Skye and Cammie spent the last few weeks pounding the pavement, getting the word out about their new business. Skye did most of the work during the week, when Cammie was busy teaching. Skye attended business fairs and seminars, shaking hands and passing out cards wherever she went.

Inserting a push-pin into the last flier on the bulletin board of the Boca Raton Club, Skye felt her stomach rumbling. "I'm hungry. Let's grab lunch." She and Cammie were out most of the morning, posting fliers and handing out business cards in ritzy hotels, government buildings, and golf courses.

"Cool." Cammie pushed a wisp of hair from her face. "There's a Chinese place around the corner."

They made the short walk from the club to the Jade Palace, and were soon seated, having loaded their plates with various offerings from the buffet.

Skye sat across from her friend in the booth they'd chosen, sipping from her glass of water. "I want to thank you again for doing this with me, Cammie."

She nodded. "It's no problem. I was tired of teaching, and this business venture will be a welcome respite from dealing with teenagers and their fickle hormones on a daily basis."

Skye laughed. "It was that bad, huh?"

"Worse." Cammie took a bite of her spring roll. "Some days I had to pry them apart because they were kissing in class, other times I had to separate them to keep them from killing each other."

"I don't want you to think of yourself as my secretary. It's true I asked you to do this because of your organizational skills, but we're partners."

Cammie winked. "I know. You certainly didn't pick me for my 'design aptitude,' I don't have any."

"Just making sure," Skye commented.

"As much as teaching irritated me, I wouldn't have quit if I thought you only wanted me as a secretary. So," Cammie said, winding lo mien noodles around her fork, "do you think we're off to a good start with the advertising?"

"I really think it's going well." Skye savored a tangy mouthful of sweet and sour shrimp, her favorite Chinese dish. "I think we've definitely generated some interest among the high end clientele we want to bring in. I think we've pretty much hit everyone in Lawrence's Rolodex."

"Lucky you married a big-time lawyer. He knows people in high places." Cammie tucked a wayward curl behind her left ear. "I feel like the radio ads I purchased will only garner more attention for us." To further ensure they attracted the business they were seeking, Cammie footed the bill for a series of radio ads, which aired on all the local classical and jazz stations. "Since the stations are owned by the university, their prices were reasonable, so we didn't break the bank." She waved her hand over her steaming cup of green tea, letting the smell waft into her nostrils before taking a long sip.

"Well," Skye smiled, lifting her glass, "it looks like our little business is off to a solid start."

Cammie raised her mug as well, and the two friends

clanked them in agreement.

Chapter 2
May 2005

On a slightly overcast mid May morning, Skye was on cloud ten. That day, Boca Interior Associates, Inc., was opening for its first official day of business. The office was in Magnolia Chase Office Park, where it occupied the entire fifth floor.

As she drove to her office, she blasted her favorite radio station, WGRV, The Groove. Skye caught a few crazy looks from other drivers as she bopped her head and sang along loudly to the hits of the early nineties, but she didn't care. She insisted her morning commute be nothing less than enjoyable.

When Skye arrived at the office, Cammie was already sitting behind the reception desk. From her attaché case, she pulled out her newly framed Associate of Arts in Interior Design degree, and showed it to Cammie.

"Very nice," Cammie commented.

"Got it framed yesterday. It's been sitting on my closet shelf for ten years now. I'm going to hang it in my office." Skye eyed her friend's gorgeously long, naturally curly brown hair, which was once again bound up in a chignon on the back of her head. "Girl, why don't you ever wear your hair down? Bundling it up like that has got to make your head heavy."

Cammie's crystal blue eyes sparkled with amusement. "A little. But it gets so frizzy in this humidity."

"That's an acceptable excuse. My second question. What are you doing here so early?"

"Well, I woke up at five thirty this morning. Wayne was

already gone, and I had nothing better to do. So I got dressed, came in early, and vacuumed the entire office." Cammie tapped a pencil on her desk. "I've been here, being productive, since seven. The question is, where have you been, Johnny-Come-Lately?"

"It's only nine, Cammie, and we don't even open until ten. You're such a nut." Skye laughed a little, noticing Cammie's outfit. "And what the hell are you wearing?"

Cammie stood up and modeled her electric green cotton pantsuit. "What, you don't like it?"

"I like it, it shows off your curves, but I didn't think you owned anything that bright. You were always wearing brown and black to school." She referred to Cammie's former job, teaching English.

"Well, it was kind of a power play. My students would never have taken me seriously if I dressed like this for class." Cammie sat down in her rolling office chair. "Besides, they probably would have given me some awful nickname, like Rainbow Bright or Green Lantern."

"Could you blame them?" Both she and Cammie laughed.

Within an hour, a petite blond entered the office. Cammie greeted her with a smile.

"Welcome to Boca Interior Associates," Cammie began. "How can I help you?"

"Oh, hello. I'm Doreen. I'm the secretary to Senator Benita York." She extended her hand, and Cammie shook it. "I'm here to set up a consultation appointment for her."

"I'll be glad to help you with that." Cammie gestured to the chair in front of the desk. "Have a seat, if you like."

While Doreen took her seat, Cammie pulled up the client database on her computer.

"Okay, Doreen," Cammie said, looking up from the screen, "I'll just need to ask you a few questions. What type of work is the Senator requesting?"

"She would like her guest bedrooms remodeled."

"How many rooms is the Senator remodeling?" Cammie typed away as she listened.

"Two. They haven't been redone in a number of years."

"What day would the Senator be available to meet with the designer?"

"She's actually on vacation this week," Doreen noted, flipping through the pages of a day planner. "She'd like to see Ms. Holdron tomorrow, if that's possible."

"Sure," Cammie agreed, still typing. "Mrs. Holdron has an opening at ten tomorrow morning."

"That's perfect. Will she be coming to the house?"

"Yes, ma'am. Just let me take down the address."

Doreen gave Cammie the home address of Senator York, then stood. "Is that all the information you need from me?"

"Yes, you're all set." Cammie rose, shaking hands with her once again. "Mrs. Holdron will see you tomorrow."

"Thanks so much," Doreen called back, making her way out of the office.

The rest of the day was uneventful, but Skye and Cammie were thrilled to have a prominent state senator as their first client.

"We hooked a pretty big fish, getting a state senator as our first client," a beaming Skye said, as she laid a stack of magazines on the reception area table. "Let's celebrate."

"Bellini it is," Cammie called out from her desk across the room.

When they left the office around six in the evening, Skye followed Cammie to the charming, family owned Italian restaurant. Seated in a quiet corner booth with their drinks, they waited for their server.

"What are you gonna have?" Cammie asked, poring over the menu.

"Veggie lasagna, I think."

"What can I get for you ladies?"

Skye and Cammie looked up. The familiar white-coated waiter, Leo, stood next to the table.

"Oh, I'll have the vegetarian lasagna, please." Skye handed him her menu.

"And I'll have the minestrone soup and antipasto."

Leo took Cammie's menu as well, and disappeared into the kitchen.

They spent dinner talking business, and enjoying each others' company. Then the two friends parted ways, each going home for the evening.

*

After Skye pulled her SUV into the garage, she entered the house. It was after seven; Lawrence should definitely be home, but the house was dark and his pickup wasn't there.

Hmm, I wonder where Lawrence could be.

As Skye moved through the house, she listened for any sign of him. She knew he could be downstairs in his office, or taking a nap on the window seat in their bedroom. As she neared the staircase, she could hear soft jazz floating toward her. The smell of vanilla wafted into Skye's nostrils and invited her up the stairs, where she followed it into their bedroom.

When Skye walked into the bedroom, she couldn't believe her eyes. The dancing flames of dozens of pillar candles illuminated the room. Skye dropped her briefcase next to the chaise and followed the trail of orange rose petals that led to the bed. The curtains were drawn but she could see Lawrence's silhouette through them. When she opened the curtains, he was reclining in the center of the bed, wearing nothing but a pair of red silk boxers and a million-dollar smile. Skye gasped.

"Hello, sweetness, how was your day?"

"Lawrence, you..." Skye stammered.

"Yeah, I know. I surprised you. I just wanted to let you know how proud I am of you on your first day of business." He kissed her gently on the lips. "I love you, girl."

Skye's eyes softened and misted at Lawrence's display of affection. "I love you."

He dipped his head and kissed her roughly, urgently. When he finally released her lips, she drew in a shaky breath.

"You look so handsome...I need this so badly."

She ran her hands lovingly over his chest. Even after ten years of marriage, Lawrence still set her blood on fire.

"I'm glad to oblige you, sexy." Lawrence dipped his head again, this time kissing a trail of pleasure down the side of her neck and onto her shoulder. Skye sighed and clung to him as his tongue traced magic patterns over her skin.

*

Without a word, he reached behind her and undid the hook and eye closure of her blouse. She lifted her arms and he removed the first barrier between them. He tossed it onto the chaise and began to kiss the exposed flesh around her lacy lavender bra. As he reached around her, he undid the bra and it soon joined her top on the chaise. Lawrence directed his attention to her nipples, sucking contentedly on each dark peak. When he gently bit her left nipple, Skye's knees buckled; he caught her and laid her on her back on their bed. With slow, tedious hands, he dragged her pants down her gorgeous brown legs, kissing and licking each revealed inch of trembling flesh. Then he peeled off her lavender panties, tossing them aside. For a moment, he froze, captivated. His eyes traveled over the smooth skin spread so beautifully over the soft curves of her body. She excited him fully.

He leaned near her ear. "Every part of you, from your full, ripe lips to your rounded hips, was made to please me."

Watching her tremble in response, his hardness grew at the thought of her legs wrapped around his waist, her tight passage squeezing and milking him of all he had.

"You are so gorgeous," he whispered.

*

As he shed his boxers and lay on top of her, she felt his demanding erection pressing against her thigh. He was as long, sturdy, and thick as a lead pipe, and Skye could not deny her need for his 'pipe laying' expertise.

He kissed her again, deeply, his hands traveling up and down her body. As he touched her, Skye shivered with desire. The moist evidence of her excitement flowed between her legs. As if in tune with her, he gently pressed his hand between her thighs at that very moment. His fingers were the keys that unlocked the gates to her secret garden. She opened to him, like a flower to the sun, and he stroked her, showing her a small preview of the bliss to come.

She knew he was well versed in pleasing her, and as he expertly teased her dewy folds, he coaxed more and more of passion's honey from her. He paid special attention to her swollen clit, massaging and squeezing the tiny bud. Then he moved inside to her G-spot, stroking the sensitive flesh in a 'come hither' motion. The rising tide of ecstasy soon became too much to bear, and she shouted in abandon. He held her as orgasm swept over her body like a wave. Through passion-hooded eyes, she could see him watching her. He kissed her gently on the forehead as the shivering and moaning subsided.

He knelt between her legs, pressing his hardness against the now slick and inviting place he prepared for his coming. The moment he entered her, their eyes locked, and they both shuddered as her body seemed to draw him in. He moved slowly, and she clung to him, her hips rising to meet his thrusts. Dipping his head low as he gyrated above her, he flicked his tongue over her already stiff nipples.

Skye groaned in rapturous delight, lifting her breasts toward his warm mouth to give him better access. She felt so many emotions; the pleasure that made her pulse race, the deep and fathomless love that led her to share her body and soul with this man, and the joy she felt that he returned her adoration. The silken whisper of mahogany flesh against bronze flesh and their moans filled the room. The rhythm built and built, until Lawrence's hips were moving so fast she thought she'd burst into flames from the sweet friction. He held back, sweat running in rivulets down his face and back, for as long as he could. The pipe layer grasped her hips and lifted them, pounding into her so deeply she could feel him in her abdomen. Soon, he was roaring as orgasm gripped him. Thrusting one last, deep thrust, he filled her with the creamy evidence of his pleasure.

*

Lawrence rose, lifted his wife, and turned back the covers. Once he laid her down, he lay next to her, pulled her into his arms, and pulled the bed linens over them. When the sun rose over the Atlantic, its rays broke through the bay window and found them, just that way, asleep, their arms wrapped around each other.

*

Lawrence's eyes opened as the loud ringing of the alarm clock filled the room. Slapping the 'off' button, he took a moment to let his eyes adjust to the sunlight, shifting a little to wake Skye. She opened her eyes, looked up and saw him, and smiled sweetly.

"Good morning."

"Good morning, baby." He kissed her forehead gently. "Get up. It's almost seven thirty."

She always looked so beautiful the mornings after they made love. Her tousled hair, sparkling eyes, and naked form brought back a rush of erotic memories. His eyes met hers, and she blushed.

"Why are you staring at me like that?"

It was all he could do not to drag her beneath the rumpled sheets and take her again. "Just glad you belong to me, that's all."

Smiling, he sat up and stretched.

*

Groggy, Skye made her way to the bathroom. Looking forward to taking a hot shower, she retrieved a towel from the built-in cabinet next to the sink, and donned her yellow floral shower cap. She was stepping into the stall when she slipped on a pair of Lawrence's underwear. With outstretched hands, she managed to steady herself on the glass door.

"UGH!" She rolled her eyes, picked up the boxers from the floor and stepped into the bedroom. When she discovered Lawrence was no longer there, she frowned.

Clutching the evidence, she stalked naked down the stairs to Lawrence's home office. Finding the door closed and locked, as she suspected, she shouted through it.

"Lawrence, could you please stop leaving your stank ass drawers on the bathroom floor? I nearly broke my damn neck!"

"Chill!" came the shouted reply from the other side of the closed door. "You survived, didn't you? Besides, I'm working on a motion here!"

"That's all you ever do!" Skye shot back. "You're always trapped in that damn office working." She sighed, shaking her head. "I don't have time for this. I've got to start on a remodel for a state senator today."

"Well, nobody's stopping you. Go do what you gotta do."

Skye all but stomped back up the stairs, leaving the dirty underwear on the office doorknob. Now she was more in need of a shower than before. I have to calm my frazzled nerves so I can concentrate on doing a great job for my first client.

Standing beneath the comforting cascade of heated water from the the multi-function detachable shower head, Skye came up with the perfect way to relax. Removing the shower head from its cradle, she turned on the concentrated spray and directed the jet of steamy water toward the tiny center of her pleasure. Moments later, her legs were trembling, threatening to give way beneath her as she rode out an intense orgasm.

Renewed, Skye dressed in a comfortable pair of brown, wide legged trousers and a black, cap sleeved, button front top. Stepping into her favorite low-heeled black mules, she grabbed her purse and the attaché case holding her design sketches.

Jogging down the steps, she noticed Lawrence was still in his office, but removed the underwear from the doorknob. Smiling, she took a banana and a travel mug of coffee from the kitchen, then left home, headed for Senator Benita York's suburban palace.

*

As Skye waited at the traffic light on Boca Raton Country Club Parkway, she put on her wireless headset and dialed the office. Cammie picked up on the third ring.

"Boca Interior Associates, this is Camilla, how may I direct your call?"

"Hey, Cammie, it's me. How's everything at the office?"

"Everything's cool. No one here except for me and the guy who delivers water. What's up?"

"I'm on my way to Senator York's place."

"Oh, yeah, I almost forgot. Terri called."

Skye knew Cammie was nervous from her tone. She was probably twisting the phone cord around her fingers.

"So, what did she want? Don't tell me she's not coming in tomorrow."

The last thing Skye needed to hear right now was that their newly hired assistant, Terri Kirk, wasn't coming in. She needed the extra hands to do the job in a timely manner, and as an interior design major, Terri needed the experience.

Cammie answered her question. "Well, she said she has to make up an exam. But she's sending someone to replace her, just for tomorrow. His name is Justin...Pope."

That's funny, Skye thought, Pope was Maurice's last name. I went to school with that wacko back at Duke. The very thought of his name made her stomach turn.

Back in the day, Maurice Pope obsessed over Skye. He went to extreme lengths to garner her affections. She glanced over her shoulder, as if checking to see if he was there.

"Well, okay. I guess we don't have any choice. Anyway, we need the extra set of hands[so I can get started tomorrow]. I'll be at the restaurant for lunch around noon. Close up shop and meet me there, okay?"

"Sure. See you then." Cammie hung up the phone.

Skye knew Cammie was watching soap operas on the small black and white TV she kept on the edge of her desk. When she wasn't watching "All My Children," she answered the phones and kept the office running, so Skye let it slide.

Skye pulled into the long, winding driveway that led to

the Senator's house. After she parked, she was met by a stern looking female security guard who waved a hand held metal detector over her, then let her pass. When she rang the doorbell, she was ushered in by an older white man.

"My name is James, Senator York's butler. Welcome, Mrs. Holdron. Senator York is waiting in her office."

James escorted Skye past the mahogany paneled walls and crystal vases to a large office behind the spiral staircase. There, behind an over-sized mahogany desk, sat the petite form of Senator Benita Menendez York.

Skye was impressed with the senator's stylish attire, a goldenrod, double-breasted pantsuit with bronze buttons. Right down to the gold rosette studs in her ears and the matching black velvet choker, Skye could see the woman exuded class and breeding. When she rose from the desk, she walked over to Skye and extended her hand.

"Mrs. Holdron," Senator York said with a slight accent, "such a pleasure to meet you."

"Likewise, Senator. I've read about your work, and I'm honored to meet someone who advocates so fiercely for women and minorities."

"Thank you. I've always been passionate about civil rights." She paused, changing the subject. "Well, as my assistant told you, I have two guest bedrooms upstairs in dire need of a makeover. I picked up one of your cards at the state capitol building, and I wanted to see your skills in action." She smiled. "So, let me show you the rooms."

Skye was again impressed, with the senator's modesty. She followed her client up the spiral staircase and into a large bedroom.

"I haven't done any decorating since John and I divorced five years ago. You probably know my ex-husband." Senator York gestured to a small, framed photo of him on the bookshelf. Skye didn't detect a hint of bitterness or sarcasm in her voice; it was obvious Benita held no ill-will for her former husband.

"Yes, I know him. John York, the biggest competition my husband's firm ever had. Whatever happened to the practice?" Skye asked. She remembered how glad Lawrence had been to see them go, and wondered where they went.

"Oh, John moved it back home to Shreveport. I hear it's doing well. What's can you do to update this room?"

Skye spent the next few hours with Senator York, ascertaining Senator York's desires for the rooms, and creating a workable budget. Around noon, James escorted her to the door.

"Thanks for your help, Mrs. Holdron," Senator York called, from the top of the stairs. "I'll see you and your assistant tomorrow, okay?"

"We'll be here around eleven, Senator. And thank you." Skye walked into the afternoon sun and climbed into her truck. Slinging her purse into the passenger seat, she started the truck and pulled out of the driveway.

Soon, she parked in a space at Bellini and dashed inside. She spotted Cammie by the coral, knee length dress and coordinating print scarf she wore. Skye joined her friend at the bar, where she was waiting, sipping a mimosa.

"Is it happy hour already?" Skye said, as she sat down on the stool next to Cammie.

"Always." Cammie giggled. "Why are you so late?"

"Ten minutes. Senator York was quite a chatterbox. But she's a delightful woman, and I love her political platform. Did you order for me?"

"You know I did. Minestrone and a salad. I'm having the same."

"Watching your figure, huh? Are you thinking you might have to get into a certain white dress sometime soon?" Skye leaned toward her.

Cammie smiled knowingly. "It's just a matter of time."

Their waiter put the soup and salad in front of them. They talked for a little while about Skye's plans for the Senator's room as they ate. Then, Skye put down her fork and turned to Cammie with a serious look on her face.

"Did you say the person who's coming to replace Terri tomorrow is named Jason Pope?"

"You got the last name right. But his first name's Justin." Cammie raised an eyebrow. "What, do you think he's related to that crazy guy from Duke?"

For a moment, Skye shivered inwardly, but tried not to appear nervous. She didn't want to alarm her friend. "Probably not; I know Pope is a common last name. Just out of curiosity," she lowered her voice, "do you still keep that Louisville Slugger bat in your trunk?"

"Hell yeah," Cammie assured her. "And I still swing away when I have to, girl."

After lunch, Cammie and Skye went to pick up some fabric and wallpaper they needed for the Senator's remodel. They entered their office building around three o'clock, chatting and laughing as they rode the elevator to the fifth floor.

"I hope Terri isn't going to make a habit of missing work. She needs this internship with us; it's a requirement for her degree." Skye fished around in her purse for the keys as they stepped off the elevator.

"I know. I hope that's motivation enough for her." Cammie smiled. "She seems really focused on her academics...hey, what's that?" Cammie pointed to the office door as they approached. "There's something taped to the door."

"Well, it better not be an eviction notice," Skye joked. "The lease is paid up for three months, and I'm not about to..."

Skye stopped dead in front of the door to Boca Interior Associates. Her keys and purse suddenly slipped from her grasp. Her breath grew rapid and labored, panic rising in her chest as she realized what was there.

"Oh my God, Skye," Cammie said urgently, as she read the tattered paper. "I'm calling security right now."

Skye was frozen in place, shaking and struggling to breathe, as Cammie grabbed her cell phone and called security. She just couldn't bring herself to open the door. Not with the omen that was stuck so haphazardly to the frosted glass.

It was a faded, worn flier, advertising the 1989 Omega Psi Phi Roll-out Party at North Carolina Central University. The word 'remember' was scribbled across it in angry red letters.

As two uniformed security guards rushed toward the office, Skye fell to the taupe carpeted floor with a heavy thud.

Chapter 3
June 2005

Skye ran hard and fast through the shadowy parking lot. Ducking the low-hanging branches of willow trees and weaving between the empty cars, she fled in panic. The student union was just ahead, full of students dancing and drinking. She headed in the direction of the old beige brick building.

But when she reached the side entrance, the door was locked from the inside. No matter how hard she tugged , it wouldn't open. The people inside just kept   dancing, oblivious to the frightened young woman trying to enter.

The loud music continued to thump as she banged and banged on the door, screaming at the top of her lungs. She yelled for help until she was hoarse. No one heeded her desperate cries.

She heard the footsteps behind her. He's coming, she thought, tears streaming down her face. Her lungs burned as she tried to catch her breath. She wanted to run, but her feet seemed frozen to the spot where she stood.

He grabbed her, spun her around, and slammed her against the brick wall.

"Uppity whore," he growled, reaching for her.

"No!" she screamed, as he took hold of her. She tried to wriggle her way out of his grasp, but he was too strong. His face was so close to her that she could smell the rancid stench of beer on his breath. Closing her eyes, she growled angrily, her fists and feet flailing as she tried to fight him off...

"Skye! Wake up, baby."

Skye opened her eyes. Lawrence gripped her shoulders, a worried look on his face. She looked around. It was after nightfall, and she was home, in her own bed.

"Oh, baby." Skye sank into his embrace. "I had that nightmare again..."

"It's okay," Lawrence kissed her forehead. "You had a panic attack and passed out at the office. The security guard revived you, I brought you home, and you've been asleep for the past three hours."

Trying to shake the cold, clammy feeling overcoming her, she cried quietly into her husband's strong shoulder.

*

As he held her, Lawrence sighed inaudibly. When is she going to deal with this? I can't protect her from the nightmares and panic attacks forever.

He'd always been there for her, and always would be, but her stubbornness was the main factor keeping her from getting over what had happened to her. Fifteen years had past, and she simply pushed the memories aside, refusing to get therapy, or even acknowledge the trauma she experienced.

In his arms, he could feel Skye begin to relax, a luxury he didn't have. He worried about her all the time. What if she had a panic attack while driving? She could be hurt, or killed.

In the settling silence, as she drifted off to sleep again, he prayed she would acknowledge the pain locked away so long ago, before something terrible happened.

*

When Skye arrived at the office, the first order of business was making sure that security was strictly enforced. After she checked the front desk of the building, she rode the elevator to her floor. She dressed down that day, wearing dark denim boot cut jeans, a red peasant blouse, and low heeled red mules. There was no need to wear a business suit for today's kind of work.

When Skye entered the office, she found Cammie at the reception desk.

"Anything strange or out of place?" Skye asked.

"No," Cammie replied, "but Justin Pope is due here any minute."

The two friends exchanged a look. Neither was able to hide their nervousness.

"Well, like I said, we'll be keeping a close eye on him." Skye sat in one of the plush chairs in the reception area and awaited Mr. Pope's arrival.

About fifteen minutes later, Justin Pope entered the office. He was a thin, young black man, around six feet tall and weighing a buck fifty. He looked nineteen, with a complexion that mimicked dark chocolate. As he stepped inside, wearing a yellow polo shirt and loose khaki pants, Cammie and Skye watched him intently. Moments passed, then Skye stood.

"Welcome. My name is Skye Holdron. You must be Justin." Skye extended her hand, and Justin shook it. He had a firm grip. She gestured to Cammie. "This is my business partner, Camilla Hamlin." She was determined to lay down the law; there was no need for him to know she and her friend were nervous. Sure, he shared a last name with someone who had once been the bane of her existence, trying to force her to love him. But there was no proof that this young man had any knowledge of Maurice.

There was only one way to find out.

"Hi, Ms. Holdron, Ms. Hamlin. Terri asked me to cover for her, just for today, so she can make up an exam." He smiled shyly. "I really don't know much about decorating.

I'm a criminal justice major. Bur I'll help as much as I can."

Skye smiled a little. "Well, I really just need an extra set of hands." She motioned to a chair. "Please, have a seat, Mr. Pope." She waited for him to sit down, and then sat across from him. Cammie stood, her tan and indigo skirt swirling as she moved to sit next to Skye.

"Now, Mr. Pope, I need to ask a few things before we go to the Senator's home," Skye began calmly. "Are you related to a Maurice Gregory Pope who attended Duke University? He's a dermatologist now."

*

Justin appeared thoughtful for a moment. The cousin of mine who asked me to watch your house? "Yes. Maurice is a second cousin of mine on my father's side. Why do you ask, Ms. Holdron?"

"Well, Justin, I attended school with your cousin. We had some contention between us, and haven't spoken in years, but suddenly, we found something threatening taped to our office door yesterday." Skye leaned forward. "We don't want to be accusatory, but..."

Cammie spoke up. "Do you know anything about this, Justin?"

How cute, they're playing detective. He had no idea when his cousin approached him weeks ago about tailing Skye that it would be this interesting. But there was no way they would ever know he was involved. After he cased the house a few times to determine when Skye would be home alone, he gave the information to Maurice, who paid his tuition all the way through senior year as payment.

When his classmate Terri asked him to cover her shift, he couldn't resist the chance to meet the famous Skye Donovan up close. She was beautiful, but he didn't see why Maurice was so enamored with her.

Oh, well. I did a little favor for Maurice, now I'll

graduate debt free.

"No, I don't, ma'am," Justin answered, in an assertive tone, putting on his best 'clueless' face. "I haven't seen my cousin since I was a kid, and I certainly would not participate in anything like that." Technically, I'm not involved, because I've already done my part.

Cammie and Skye looked at Justin, then at each other.

"Well," Cammie began, "you seem to be a responsible young man, and we are willing to give you the benefit of the doubt. However, I'm sure you understand why we had to ask."

Skye stood again. "We will pay you for your work, Justin. Please understand that this does not reflect badly on your personal character, but we would prefer it if you didn't cover for Terri again."

"Certainly, Ms. Holdron. I wouldn't want you uncomfortable. This is just a favor for a friend." Justin shook his head. "Whatever the problem is between you and Maurice, I would like to distance myself from it."

After their conversation, Skye drove to Senator York's home, with Justin following her. Once they arrived and brought their equipment into the larger of the two rooms, Skye turned to Justin.

"I'd like you to start by steaming off this awful floral wallpaper," Skye gestured to the steaming machine. "Meanwhile, I'm going to pull up the carpet and see what's underneath."

As Skye knelt near the room's doorway with a carpenter's knife, she stripped away the heavy staples holding the carpet to the floor. Pulling back the aging Berber, she gasped.

"Wow," she said aloud.

Justin, who was steaming the eastern wall of the room, glanced in her direction. "What is it?"

"There are some absolutely beautiful mahogany floors

under here." She mused momentarily. "I'll change my design slightly to accommodate this pleasant surprise."

Around six, their work for the day completed. Even though Skye had seen a fleeting look of guilt when she and Cammie questioned Justin, there was no reason to believe he'd been lying. She pushed aside her suspicions, shook his hand, paid him, and watched his 1997 Escort wagon as it disappeared down Senator York's winding driveway. Skye heaved a sigh of relief and left, speeding toward home and the comfort of Lawrence's arms.

*

Lawrence was on the couch, watching the evening news. He had removed his sport coat and tie, and was enjoying an ice cold beer when the phone rang. Reaching to the side table, he picked up the cordless phone.

"Hello?"

"Hey, Larry, How are things?" Lawrence immediately recognized the voice of his older brother, Jasper.

"Damn it; stop calling me Larry, boy! What's up?"

"Nothing much here. I don't think there's any talent left in Miami," Jasper said ruefully.

Lawrence shook his head. Jasper was always complaining, either about his job as a record company talent agent, or his fiery Japanese-American wife, Kyoko. "What happened to that rapper you were telling me about... what was his name, Glock or 380 or something like that?"

"Close. His name was M-16. Supposedly, his flow had 'firepower.' Turns out he just had a tough look with weak rhymes." Jasper laughed. "I should let you listen to the demo tape he gave me. I've heard better rapping at high school talent shows."

"Well, maybe there's another rapper out there with some real talent. Don't give up, Jasper." Lawrence changed the channel to ESPN. "Where are you, anyway?"

Jasper sighed. "I'm back in Miami now, but I just got back from the Keys. Kyoko called me every five seconds to see what I was doing. She's pissed because I didn't invite her on the trip. She probably thinks I'm cheating."

"Are you?" Lawrence already knew the answer to that. He just wanted to see if Jasper was going to lie about it.

"Yeah, but she don't know that," he scoffed. "She's supposed to trust me, isn't she? Anyway, if she stopped questioning me all the time..."

"I'm not about to have this conversation with you. Give me a call when you get yourself together, all right?" Lawrence rolled his eyes, amazed at his brother's absolute selfishness and stupidity. If Kyoko found out, Jasper would be lucky to survive her wrath with his face intact.

"All right, Law. I'll hit you back later." Jasper hung up his end of the line, and Lawrence placed the phone in the cradle as he went back to watching the news.

After he had hung up with Lawrence, Jasper motioned to Candy, the twenty-year-old blond sitting in the overstuffed armchair across from him.

He'd known he wouldn't score any points with Lawrence by being honest about his infidelity, but he needed to brag to somebody. Otherwise, there would be no way to soothe his insecurities about his manhood. "Now, where were we?"

The room was soon filled with her girlish giggles as Jasper prepared his young, naive prey for the taking.

She was the flavor of the week, but she didn't need to know that. As he kissed her neck and grazed his hands over her pert little breasts, he filled her ear with sweet words, making her swoon.

Jasper led Candy to the plush bed in the center of the room. She was young and eager, just the way he liked them. Candy was the new intern for A&R at Prime

Records, where he worked. She looked up to him as an experienced lover, a man of the world. In those twinkling blue eyes of hers, he saw all the admiration that had long since faded from his wife's gaze.

He freed her of the hot pink mini dress she wore, and let his eyes linger over the tight little body wrapped in lacy hot pink lingerie, and sighed with contentment. He ran a questing hand up Candy's thigh.

What my wife doesn't know won't hurt her.

Chapter 4
July 2005

Friday afternoon Lawrence showed up at Boca Interior Associates with Skye's bags packed and in hand. As he entered the lobby, he saw Skye sitting on the edge of Cammie's desk, conversing. Surprised to see him, she slid off the desk and walked over to him, giving him a peck on the cheek.

"Lawrence, what are you doing here?" Skye eyed the two suitcases he was carrying. "And what are you doing with my luggage?"

"You need a break, and I'm going to see that you get one. We're going to Miami to visit my dad for the weekend." He gestured to the bags. "I packed these for you so you wouldn't have to worry about it. And so you'd have no excuses to get out of this."

Thinking for a moment, Skye agreed. "I guess I could use a break. I'm game. Just give me a few minutes to lock up."

"Okay." Lawrence took a seat on the nearest cerulean micro fiber armchair in the lobby. "I'll be waiting."

Within the hour, Lawrence and Skye were on the road to Miami. When they arrived that evening, Dad was sitting out on the front porch in his weathered oak rocker.

"Hey, young fella," Theodore called out to his son. "I see you're still goin' around with this sweet Carolina girl."

"Yeah, Pop, I sure am." Lawrence smiled as he reached the porch. Leaning down, he hugged his sixty-eight year old father. "How have you been?"

"Pretty good for a young fella." Laughter lit his

wisdom-filled brown eyes.

Lawrence laughed. His father had been responding the same way to that question for at least twenty years. "Dad, you know you're going white around the temples, don't you?"

He raked an aged, arthritic hand through his thinning gray Afro. "That don't mean nothin'. Age is just a state of mind, boy." His gaze landed on his daughter in law. "And hello to you, miss." He extended his hand to Skye, who leaned down and kissed him on the cheek. "You still got the sweetest sugar of anybody I know, except for my Nancy Lee."

Lawrence stiffened at the mention of his late mother's name. His parents were married for more than forty years, and had been madly in love until the day his mother died in 1999. Though he and Jasper missed her, they knew their grief could never match Dad's. He would often say, "The day my sweet Nan died, I died some, too."

Skye spoke quietly. "Hey, Theo. I hope we gave you enough notice before we came down here."

"Oh, ain't no problem." Theodore made a sweeping motion with his hand. "I'm glad you all could come. You just stay on in Lawrence's room like usual."

*

As the three walked into the house, Theodore and Skye sat down in the living room while Lawrence went upstairs to put down their bags. They sat in silence for a few moments, and then Theodore spoke.

"Did I ever tell you how I met Nancy Lee, Skye?"

"Sure, but it's been awhile. Tell me again."

His old eyes shone with the glow of happy memories as he began.

June 1954
Fort Benning, GA

The very green, nineteen year old Private Theodore Holdron from Naples, Florida, walked into Dillard's Shop N' Save, his mouth as dry as heavy grain sandpaper. The store was located just outside the Phenix Highway gate of Fort Benning, where he was in his last week of Pathfinder school. He had intended on going straight to the cooler to procure a cola, but was stopped in his tracks by the arresting beauty of the young woman who greeted him from behind the counter.

"Welcome to Dillard's. Can I help you find anything, sir?" Her voice was as refreshing as cool water flowing over his sweat-dampened brow. Her curvy, hazelnut frame was draped in a light blue work dress with a sharply pressed white collar. The bouffant hairstyle she wore was accented by the fresh white gardenia perched behind her right ear. In his love-weakened state, he was barely able to make out the name on the tag she was wearing: Nancy.

"I...I..." It was all too much for a young Army Private on his first weekend pass to process. "I came in here for a cold drink, but I think I found my wife instead."

Nancy giggled, revealing her dazzling smile. "Oh, really?"

"Really." Theodore approached the counter and took her sweet smelling hand into his. "Marry me, Nancy. If this ain't love that I'm feeling, then you better call me an ambulance, 'cause I'm going to meet Jesus real soon."

"I suppose my Pa would be pretty upset if I married you before we even went on a date," Nancy said, blushing. "But since you're so cute, I'll let you take me down to Foley's for a root beer float. We'll see where it goes from there."

The look in her eyes told him he had a chance with her. Smiling a goofy smile, Theodore let Nancy lead him to the cooler.

"Now," she cooed, "let's see about that cold drink you wanted."

Right then and there, Theodore Holdron's heart melted into his spit-shined boots.

July 2005

"We married in May of 'fifty-six, right there in the chapel, and I never looked at no other woman in the forty-three years we were married." Theodore dreamily looked out the window, as if he was picturing Nancy's face. "She was my prize, my doll. Not a day goes by I don't miss her. But I know I'll see her again soon enough."

Skye nodded. She shared in the sadness she saw in the old man's eyes, but also in his hope of being reunited with his soul mate.

Theodore continued, "While we're talking about love, you wouldn't believe what your brother-in-law done to that poor wife of his."

Lawrence, having returned from stowing their luggage, appeared at his father's armchair with a look of worry on his face. He had come back downstairs while Theodore and Skye were talking. "What did he do, Pops?"

He shook his head. "It's a damn shame. That girl called me last night, crying and carrying on. That fool brother of yours was in their bed with some white girl when she came home from work. I know I raised both of you better than that."

Skye glanced at Lawrence, and found him frowning.

Theodore continued. "She said he acted like he didn't even care he was caught, and that the girl tried to psychoanalyze her, while wearing her good bed sheet."

Skye shook her head. "Wow. That's pretty tacky."

Lawrence asked, "Where is he, Pops?"

"Over at the Martindale Inn on Miami Boulevard. He ain't welcome in his own home." He paused. "I don't know what it is about that boy. Ever since he was a teenager, he been mounting everything on two legs in a skirt."

Lawrence grabbed his keys. "Skye, I'll be back in a few hours, baby. You and Pops chill out for awhile."

Skye exchanged a knowing look with Theodore, then pecked Lawrence on the cheek. "Okay. Don't kill him."

Lawrence dashed out of the house, cranked his truck, and sped toward the hotel. When he arrived, he stopped at the front desk and showed the clerk his driver's license.

"I'm looking for Jasper Holdron. He's my brother."

"Okay, sir." He searched briefly on the hotel computer. "He's in room three twenty-one..." Before he could say anything more, Lawrence was sprinting down the hall.

When he got off the elevator on the third floor, Lawrence pounded on the door of room 321. "I know you're in there, Jasper. Open this door."

Jasper laughed bitterly. "Why should I? So you can lecture me? Pop already did that. Go away."

Lawrence continued to pound on the door. "Look, Jasper. I don't have anything but time on my hands. We can do this all day. But it will go a lot faster if you open the door."

The door squeaked as Jasper reluctantly let him in. When he looked at him, Lawrence saw Jasper had been drinking, and that he had a black eye.

"You look like death warmed over, J." Lawrence sat down on the love seat, brushing beer cans out of his way. "Now where in the hell do you get off doing this to Kyoko?"

Jasper hung his head. "I know, I know. It was trifling. I just couldn't help it."

Lawrence laughed. "Couldn't help it? What kind of a man are you? Is that all the self-control you have? I mean, I thought I was the baby, and here I am trying to help you exercise your common sense."

Jasper dropped heavily into a nearby armchair. "I've been doing this for a long time. I just brought it to the house, well, because I wanted her to catch me."

Lawrence's eyes widened. "What? Why? You are so nasty you make me sick."

"Look, Law. I love Kyoko. I really do. I just don't get why she loves me the way she does. I'd rather be divorced than constantly wondering when she's going to come to her senses and leave me. I mean, look at her. She's so beautiful, so smart. Why would she want a man like me, six years older, who doesn't make much more money than she does?" He dropped his face into his hands. "But I didn't know it would be so bad. I hate to see her cry. I deserve the black eye she gave me."

Lawrence stood over his older brother, shaking his head. "Jasper, you know what you did was wrong. It's so wrong she may never forgive you. You brought some chick into your house and laid with her in the same bed you lay in with your wife. That's pretty nasty. And now I know why you did it, which makes it even worse." He paused, noticing the fat tears rolling down his brother's cheeks. "I know you feel guilty. But the way you feel doesn't begin to cover the betrayal she must feel. You've got to stop being so selfish, Jasper."

Jasper looked up, his eyes red and wet. "Do you think I can ever get her back?"

Lawrence sighed. "Well, anything's possible. But you better make whatever you plan on doing really good, or I'll be representing her in the divorce settlement." He sat down on the floor next to the chair. "We're going to have to figure out how to fix this mess." Producing a handkerchief from his shirt pocket, he handed it to his wayward brother.

"I don't even know where to start," Jasper said sincerely, wiping his eyes.

"First of all, you've got to agree to go to therapy with her." Sensing his brother's intention to protest, he raised his finger. "There's no way around it, Jasper. What you've done has caused a huge rift in your relationship with Kyoko. Therapy could be the only viable way to close it."

"I'm not trying to tell my business to some complete stranger. Besides, they always take the woman's side." Jasper balled up the handkerchief, tossing it back to Lawrence, who sighed loudly.

"Oh, Jasper, you big bald girl. Do you want her back or not?"

Jasper's eyes softened. "More than anything."

Lawrence placed a hand on his shoulder. "Then I suggest you quit whining, call your wife, and tell her you'll do whatever it takes to fix your marriage."

"She hasn't been taking any of my calls." His face fell, his expression turning morose again.

"Can you blame her? If you want her to know you're willing to work things out, I suggest you leave her a message. Write letters. Do what you have to do, Jasper. For once in your life, take responsibility for your actions."

"You're right." A renewed determination came over Jasper's face. "I have to do whatever it takes."

Lawrence nodded approvingly. "Now, let's go get something to eat."

Chapter 5
July 2005

As the sweltering Florida June faded into the equally scorching July, business remained steady at the design firm. Skye and Terri had finished Senator York's guest rooms, and she was so pleased she steered some of her friends in Skye's direction. With business booming and no more unpleasantness, Skye felt renewed.

Skye and Cammie were both swamped with work, and it became necessary to hire another assistant. Thursday, the sixth of July, Skye was sitting in her office, interviewing a young woman named Annette Shelton. Looking up at the well-dressed, fair haired, young woman from the neatly prepared resume she presented, Skye nodded with approval.

"Miss Shelton, I must say that I am very impressed with your resume. I see that you're an architectural engineering major, and your grades are impeccable."

"I've been interested in architecture and design since I was a child," Annette gushed. "My father is a draftsman."

"Well, we could use a bright young woman like you on our staff. Can you start Monday?"

"Sure!" Annette's green eyes shone with excitement as she stood and extended her hand. "Thank you, Mrs. Holdron. I'll be here bright and early Monday morning."

"Thank you, Miss Shelton." Skye shook her hand heartily.

"Oh, please call me Annette."

"One more thing before you leave, Annette." Skye punched the intercom button on her desk phone. "Terri, could you please come to my office?"

Moments later, Skye's assistant appeared in the doorway. "Yes, ma'am?"

"I just wanted you to meet Annette. She'll be starting Monday as our new design assistant."

The two young women shook hands politely.

"Welcome to the team, Annette." Terri eyed Annette's dangling butterfly earrings. "By the way, I love those earrings."

"Thanks. I made them." Annette returned Terri's friendly smile. "I could make you some, if you want."

"I'd like that."

As Skye watched, her two assistants walked out of her office together, chatting like old friends.

Cammie stuck her head in the office door. "Wow. Terri and Annette sure have hit it off."

Skye nodded. "I noticed, and I'm glad. I'm not into refereeing cat-fights, you know. Oh, I almost forgot to tell you. I've contracted a painting company to do all of our painting. It's a local company called True Colors."

"Good. That will save us the hassle of trying to contract a company for each job separately, or from trying to paint ourselves." Cammie shook her head. "Trust me; you don't want me anywhere near a paintbrush."

Giggling, Cammie returned to her desk in the lobby. Within ten minutes, she returned.

"What is it?" Skye looked up from the sketch she was working on.

"The mailman dropped off the mail." She placed the stack on Skye's desk. "The top one looks like the bank statement on our business account." Cammie sat on the edge of the desk, drumming her fingers with expectancy. "Well, aren't you going to open it?"

Skye used the plastic opener on her desk to open the envelope. Taking the statement out, she scanned the numbers it displayed. "Well, Cammie, it looks like our bank account runneth over. We're seventeen thousand in the black!"

"Wow," Cammie slid off the desk's edge. "That's a pretty good return on our investment. And we've only been in business a few months."

"Now that you've heard the numbers, are you gonna wait around for me to open all the mail, or can I go back to my sketches?"

Cammie slapped Skye playfully on the top of the head. "Go back to your work, girl. I just wanted to know how our bank account was faring." She waved as she disappeared down the hall.

Friday morning, Skye came into the office at a quarter to nine. She was surprised to see that, for the first time, she had beaten Cammie to work. As she unlocked the office and stepped inside, she noticed how oddly quiet the office was. The click of her stilettos echoed on the marble floor as she walked toward her private office. When she opened the door, she noticed the message light blinking on her desk phone. Skye dropped her briefcase and purse next to the leather swivel chair, sat down, and pushed the blinking button.

A familiar male voice filled the room "Mrs. Holdron, this is Mark Dowdy at True Colors. I just wanted to let you know that we'll need to redo the job at Dale Winthorpe's house. Mrs. Winthorpe has changed her mind about the color. She called us directly, so we'll just bill her directly. If you have any questions, just give me a call."

As he recited the phone number, Skye jotted it onto a sticky note and stuck it to the monitor of her computer.

A chime signaled the end of the first message, followed by a beep to signal the beginning of the next. The female voice on the tape was familiar, but Skye couldn't place it.

"Skye. This is an old friend. Hope you got my little

message last month. We wouldn't want you getting forgetful..."

Skye's eyes widened with horror as the caller continued.

"Sorry I missed you. I know you aren't in the office, I watched you leave a few minutes ago. I just wanted to let you know we haven't forgotten, and we're not going to let you."

The recording ended with a click. As the machine recited the time and date, Skye sat listening. Nervousness rose unbidden inside of her. Yesterday at six thirty-six? Somebody was watching me!

Skye was reaching for the phone to call security when it rang. With a slow, shaking hand, she picked up the receiver.

"Hello?"

"Hey, sis, what's happening?" Much to Skye's irritation, it was her twenty-six year old younger sister, Delva, calling from Fort Lauderdale. "Why do you sound so weird?"

"DiDi, I'll have to call you back. And who gave you my office number?"

"I called your house, Lawrence gave it to me. What's eating you, anyway?"

"Someone is threatening me, DiDi. I think it might be Pope."

"Who? That guy who went to Duke with you? Why?"

"I can't explain right now. I've got to go. I'll call you back." Skye hung up before Delva had the chance to speak again and rushed downstairs to the security desk.

When Cammie arrived, Skye was waiting for her with the security guard and Thursday's surveillance tape.

*

That evening, Jasper and Kyoko went for their first therapy session with Dr. Tristan J. Ellis, PhD, one of the most reputable marriage counselors in Florida. Kyoko sat next to Jasper on the leather sofa and looked into the soulful eyes of the man she married. She recalled the three weeks of messages he left her, begging for forgiveness. He sent her so many bouquets that the kitchen could double as a flower shop. After all his pleading, she decided to give Jasper a second chance. Kyoko sighed, hoping she wouldn't regret her choice.

"So, Mr. and Mrs. Holdron, why are you here?" The tall, dark skinned Dr. Ellis crossed his legs and waited for a response. Kyoko spoke first, quietly.

"Doctor, less than a month ago, I came into our home and found my husband in our bed with some white girl who looked about nineteen." She could still see them there, defiling her bed; the pain was very present and real.

"Hmm. Well, Mrs. Holdron, that must have been very painful for you." Dr. Ellis leaned forward. "Is it the fact that she was younger, or that she was white, that hurts you the most?"

"Neither." Kyoko struggled with the words. "What hurt...was that there was another woman in my bed. I felt betrayed, dirty, used. He did not even try to explain himself." Tears slid down her cheeks, and Dr. Ellis handed her a box of tissues.

He turned to Jasper. "Well, Mr. Holdron, why did you do this hurtful thing to your wife?"

Jasper looked at the floor, ashamed. "I don't know why she loves me, Doc. So I figured that if I did this, she would divorce me, and I wouldn't have to live with the fear anymore."

"What fear?" Dr. Ellis prodded.

"The fear that one day she would find someone younger, better looking, wealthier, and walk out on me. I'd rather push her away..."

"Before you get hurt," Dr. Ellis finished Jasper's

statement.

"Yes. That's the truth." Jasper turned to Kyoko. "But if I had known it would hurt you so much, I would never have done it. I'm so sorry, Ky. Please forgive me." His eyes were more sincere at that moment than she had ever seen them.

Kyoko could barely see through her tears. "Jasper, I still love you. But you hurt me so badly I wanted to lie down and die. How can I ever trust you again after you did something so selfish and cruel?"

Jasper dropped to his knees in front of her. "Ky, please. I'll do anything. Don't leave me. I can't live without you. I love you too much to let you walk away." He grabbed her hand and held it tightly to his chest. "Just tell me what I have to do to get you back."

She looked into his red-rimmed eyes. "Jasper, you have to keep seeing Dr. Ellis with me until we work through all of our issues. And you have to see someone about your self esteem issues." She touched his face and leaned closer to him. "And you'll have to live with the fact that I don't trust you, until you can earn my trust back." There would be no lovemaking anytime soon, not until she could purge the image of Jasper giving what was meant for her to someone else.

"Fine. Whatever you want. I love you, Ky." Jasper returned to his seat next to her and reached for her. For the first time in weeks, Kyoko let Jasper touch her. He held her close and let her cry on his silk shirt.

"I love you..." Kyoko's words broke up her sobbing. "It just hurts so badly..."

Dr. Ellis sat back in his chair. "Well, Mr. Holdron, if you are sincere in your promises, we can work through these issues, and I can refer you to an excellent psychotherapist."

She could feel Jasper's embrace tightening. He stroked

her hair, and the sensation was like a whispered promise.

"I am sincere, Doc" he said. "For the first time in a long time."

*

Cammie came home that night from the office exhausted. The police spent most of the day at BIA, attempting to figure out who left the threatening message on Skye's voice mail. The security tape had shown a woman using a pay phone near the parking deck, but the camera was too far away to capture a clear image of her face. They were no closer to identifying her when Cammie left.

Cammie entered her house and plopped down on the couch, kicking off her white flats. She noticed how quiet the house was as she flipped on the television. Wayne must be out somewhere.

Before long, Cammie fell asleep on the couch. Only the sound of Wayne's key in the lock roused her from her catnap. Opening her eyes, she saw Wayne standing over her, smiling. She drank in his tall, rugged good looks, his chin length blond hair and striking blue eyes. He was wearing his typical lumberyard apparel -- a red plaid shirt and blue jeans.

"Hey, Cam."

"Hey, Wayne." Cammie giggled at his ridiculousness. Her name was already abbreviated; he was the only person she knew who insisted on shortening it even further. "Where have you been?"

"Running errands." Wayne dropped his solitary shopping bag on the coffee table and sat down next to her. "You look tired. What happened at the office today?"

As Wayne rubbed her tense, aching shoulders, Cammie related the strange events.

"Someone left a threatening message on Skye's answering machine, and it sounds like the person was watching us leave the office yesterday." Cammie cooed as Wayne's magic fingers massaged away the knot in her left shoulder. "Things are really getting creepy around there."

"Hmmm...and nobody knows who left the message?"

"Nope." Cammie sighed. "I am so tired of all this drama."

"Well, maybe I can brighten up your day a little." Wayne smiled, and Cammie reciprocated.

"You always do, Wayne." Cammie looked at Wayne's Cheshire Cat grin and knew he was up to something. What is he plotting?

"I think I can do even better."

Cammie watched, without a clue, as Wayne fiddled around in his shirt pocket. Eventually, he pulled out a red velvet box. When he opened it, Cammie gasped at the half-carat diamond set on a white gold band. "Camilla Louise Hamlin, will you marry me?"

Cammie jumped off the couch, dragged Wayne into her arms, and kissed him. "Yes, Wayne Lester Wright. I will." They stood there a good five minutes, just kissing and holding each other. Wayne finally pulled away and slipped the ring on her finger.

"I hoped you'd say yes, or else I would have wasted my money on this." He pulled a lacy red teddy out of the shopping bag. "Is there any way I could convince you to wear this for me?" The mischievous sparkle in his blue eyes stoked the fire inside his bride-to-be.

Cammie smiled wickedly. "I'm two steps ahead of you." She took the flimsy garment from his hand and walked toward the bedroom. "I'll call you when I'm ready, Wayne." With that, she strutted into their bedroom and closed the door behind her.

Fifteen minutes later, Cammie called out to him. When

he entered the room, he found her draped casually across the armchair in the corner, wearing the red teddy and a pair of red heels. Wayne drew in a breath.

Cammie feigned coyness. "Ready for me?"

*

Wayne came to her like a tide to the shore. He knelt in front of the chair, as if praying to her femininity, letting his rough hands glide over her softness. He felt his arousal building as he loosened all the tiny pearl buttons running down the front of the teddy. When the garment was open, he stripped it away from her body, leaving her naked, except for the heels. Slowly, skillfully, Wayne rose just enough to kiss the peaks of her breasts, drawing them into his mouth until they were as plump and firm as summer raspberries. As she sighed, he raised her legs, draped one over each arm of the chair, and slipped his hand between them.

"Wayne..." she whispered, as he circled his finger around the fleshy nubbin sheltered there. When she was close to the edge, his mouth replaced his fingers, slowly suckling at the blood-filled center of her universe.

Cammie's back arched as she gave herself over to the sensations. The fiery ministrations of his mouth threatened to reduce her to a puddle on the floor. Her hands found the back of his head and she laced her fingers in his hair, pulling him deeper into the garden of her femininity. He stayed there, licking and kissing and loving her thoroughly, finally dipping his tongue inside her. Soon, the dam broke and she climaxed with an ecstatic cry.

Usually, he would have led her to the bed. Now, the fragrant scent of her dewy passage and the sight of her sweetness running down the tempting folds of her full behind compelled him to do otherwise. He pulled her to stand on shaky legs, sat down in the chair and pulled her into his lap. Cammie obeyed willingly and straddled him. They fumbled around until Wayne found her moist opening, then she sank easily onto his hardness. She moved, gripping Wayne's shoulders and whimpering with pleasure. He watched her buxom breasts bounce rhythmically, and he knew he could not hold back. He thrust up, impaling her deeper, deeper still, until he was almost throwing her off. Holding her full hips in his calloused hands, he bore into her like a jackhammer on asphalt until her body shook with an orgasm. Soon he erupted inside her, roaring like a wild animal at the much-needed release. Cammie collapsed onto Wayne, his softening manhood still inside her, and tried to catch her breath.

"Wayne, what..." she started.

"Shhh." She was too much woman; to enjoy her fully he had to take her again. Wayne caressed her back. "Just go with it."

Without withdrawing, he stood up. Cammie wrapped her legs around him, and as he pressed her against the closet door and began to thrust, her words turned to moans.

Chapter 6
July 2005

On the last Monday in July, Skye was in her office doing paperwork when Cammie called her from the reception desk.

"Yes, Cammie."

"Your sister's here. Can I send her in?"

"Go ahead." What the hell is she doing here? Skye braced herself, trying to hide her irritation at her sister's rudeness. She loved to show up uninvited, and drama was always in tow.

A few seconds later, Skye watched her younger sister, Delva Denise Donovan, walk in. Well, if it isn't the fashion plate. Skye eyed her sister's all black ensemble -- knee length dress, high heels, and black purse. Skye stifled a giggle when she saw the large black hat perched on her sister's head. It looked wider than Delva was tall.

"That is some getup, Delva."

Delva removed her shades slowly, as if it were a dramatization of an actual event. "All the better to mourn the tragic loss of your youth, older sister. After all, you are nine years my senior...as in senior citizen." Smiling, she sat down in front of Skye's desk, crossing her bare legs.

"Delva, take off that church hat. It's blocking the sun. Where are you headed next? A funeral in Palm Beach?"

Delva rolled her eyes, but complied. "Now what is all this nonsense about somebody stalking you?"

"It's not nonsense," Skye said, between clenched teeth. "I've been getting threats ever since the first week we opened. Frankly, I'm getting tired of it."

"So," Delva leaned forward, "what does all this mean?"

"I don't know. I just don't feel safe. Something strange is going on. I won't be able to concentrate on my work until this mess is over."

Delva laughed, waving her hand dismissively. "Couldn't this be one of your friends or an old coworker from Fitzpatrick playing a prank?"

"I really don't think so, D," Skye countered, unable to conceal her annoyance. "Don't belittle my fears. There's something serious happening, and I'm going to get to the bottom of it."

"Meanwhile, older sister, who's going to run your business? What's going to happen here while you're out playing detective?" Delva scoffed and replaced her hat, checking the hand mirror in her purse for the perfect tilt. "You are so ridiculous. Get yourself a bodyguard if you're so nervous."

"Look, glamor puss. I want your pampered ass out of my office. I don't have time for this right now. I've got things to do." Skye motioned toward the door and went back to her paperwork. Delva rose from her chair, frowning and clutching her bag.

"Well, I'll have you know I took time off from work. So I'll be here all week." She headed toward the door, and then turned in the doorway. "I'll see you tonight at your house for dinner, around nine. Ciao, Bella." She replaced her shades and left.

As Skye listened to Miss Hell on Heels marching down the hall, she shook her head.

"That girl gets on my last damn nerve," she said to no one in particular, then returned to the stack of invoices she had been going over.

After she was sure Delva was gone, Skye walked down the hall to reception desk, where she found Cammie poring over a bridal magazine. When Cammie saw Skye, she got a guilty look on her face and started to close the magazine.

"No, Cammie. Go ahead. There's nothing going on right now." Skye smiled and sat on the edge of the desk. "Besides, you don't have much longer to pick out a dress if you're getting married on New Year's Eve."

Cammie nodded. "I know, don't remind me. I'm already starting to feel the pressure. So, what did Delva want?"

"Nothing. She just came to be nosy and insult me. Worst of all, she'll be here all week, and she invited herself over to my house for dinner tonight. I hope Lawrence feels like cooking."

"It's just Delva. Call Chow Fun's and order takeout," Cammie said, as she continued to thumb through the magazine. "Whatever you feed her, you know she'll be two things -- ungrateful and unimpressed."

"Cammie, you are so right. God, I can't stand her. She was always trying to outdo me. When we were kids, everything was a competition, from hopscotch to hairdos." She paused, shaking her head. "What time is it, anyway?"

Cammie glanced at her watch. "Quarter till five."

Skye rose from the desk and turned toward her office. "I think I'm going home early. I'll finish those invoices really quick. I have a headache the size of Guam. If anybody calls or comes in, tell them they can reach me tomorrow, okay?"

"Sure, I'll lock up. Go on home." Cammie smiled at her friend. "You look like you could use the rest."

"Thanks, Cammie."

Skye returned to her office to finish her work. By ten after five, she was pulling out of the parking deck, headed home. On the way, she picked up her cell phone and called Lawrence.

He picked up on the second ring. "Hello?"

"Lawrence, it's me."

"What is it? Did something else happen? Are you okay?"

"Nothing like that. I have a colossal headache, and I wanted to let you know I'm on my way. Oh yeah, Delva is coming over for dinner at nine."

Lawrence was rolling his eyes, she could almost see it. "What the hell is she doing in town?'

"I'm starting to think she's here just to work my nerves. She came by the office and pretty much made fun of this whole crazed stalker situation. I just really need a hot bath and a nap before she descends upon us."

"I understand. I should be home in about thirty minutes. I'm on the other end of Camino Real and traffic is a pain in the ass right now. But if you get there first, wait for me, and I'll join you in that hot bath."

Skye smiled. "That's the best offer I've had all day. I'll see you in a few minutes. I love you."

"Love you too, Skye. Bye."

Twenty minutes later, Skye arrived home. She parked the car in the garage and quickly ran upstairs. There, she dropped her briefcase in the master bedroom and went into the master bath. She filled the whirlpool tub with bath beads, white rose petals, and hot water. Skye kicked aside yet another pair of her husband's dirty underwear as she stepped in, but was too tired to fuss about it. By the time Lawrence entered the bathroom, she was reclining in the sweet-smelling water waiting for him. Vanilla candles were lit along the windowsill and the double sink.

*

Lawrence smiled as he shed his Armani suit and shoes. He slipped into the tub next to his wife and kissed her lips.

"Feeling better, baby?"

"A little."

"Let's see what I can do to make things right."

Lawrence wet a lavender washcloth and soaped it with a bar of Dove. Steam rose from it as he gently bathed her arms and chest. Instructing her to lay back, he laid another warm cloth on her forehead and continued to cleanse her body. They stayed in the tub until the water was tepid, bathing in their intimacy, enjoying each others' affection. When they emerged, they were both sweet smelling and relaxed.

"It's six thirty-five," Skye said, glancing at the wall clock. "We can get in a good nap and still have time to call Chow Fun's before Miss Thing gets here. Why does she have to be so damn uppity?"

"I don't know. That's just the way she is. We just have to love her and leave it at that." Lawrence dried Skye off, then himself, and lay down on the bed. Skye gazed lovingly at his taut, naked body before joining him in bed.

He pulled her close and nuzzled into her. "Hmmm. You are always so soft after a bath like that."

Before long, they were both snoring.

*

Skye woke around eight fifteen. She sat up, feeling refreshed, but nowhere near ready to deal with her sister. She tapped Lawrence's shoulder until he opened his eyes.

"Is it time already?" he asked groggily.

"Yeah. I'll call Chow Fun's. You get dressed." Skye grabbed the phone next to the bed and dialed the restaurant.

"Chow Fun."

"Yes, I'd like to place an order for delivery. Let me have a large shrimp lo mien, small crab Rangoon, and a large sweet and sour shrimp." If I have to endure dinner with my sister, at least I should get to eat what I like. "I'll pay by credit." She fished her credit card out of her wallet and recited the number.

While she ordered, Lawrence dressed a few feet away from her. He put on a baggy pair of dark denim jeans and a bright red T-shirt, emblazoned with the face of Fat Albert. Donning his house shoes, he went downstairs.

After she hung up, Skye dressed in a mint green sun dress and a pair of matching flats. She brushed her hair into a ponytail at the crown and secured it with a sterling silver hair clip.

While Skye made the bed, the doorbell rang. Lawrence padded to the door. "Who is it?"

"Chow Fun delivery," the heavily accented female voice on the other side answered.

Lawrence opened the door, and a young woman wearing a black jacket and baseball cap with "Chow Fun" embroidered on them handed him two large plastic bags.

"Duck sauce, soy sauce, utensils in the bag," she recited, as she produced a receipt from her jacket pocket. "Have a nice night."

Lawrence handed the young woman a five dollar bill. "You do the same."

She smiled and walked away. Lawrence closed the door and made his way to the kitchen to unpack the steaming hot food. As he opened the maple cabinet over the sink in search of plates, the doorbell chimed once again.

This time, he opened the door and looked down into Delva's expectant face. "Hey, Delva, how are you?" He held back a chuckle, amused by her outfit.

"I'm very well, Lawrence. Thanks so much for inquiring." Delva sashayed into the house and dropped her bag on the coffee table. "And where is my dear older sister?"

"She's upstairs. She'll be down in a minute. Have a seat."

Delva perched primly on the edge of the beige damask sofa and laid her large hat beside her. "So, Lawrence, how are things at the firm?"

"Very well. I just closed a divorce case out of Fort Lauderdale, actually. I represented a scorned husband, and was able to keep his cheating wife from bankrupting him."

Delva scoffed, waving her perfectly manicured pink nails in the air. "Nonsense. If she cheated, he must not have been up to par in bed. He owes her for that. It takes a lot of effort and acting prowess to fake it all the time."

Lawrence rolled his eyes. "You would say something like that, Delva. But there was documented proof of five separate affairs, and just because she may have been dissatisfied, that doesn't give her the right to disrespect her husband and their vows," he replied tightly. He was once again amazed by Delva's small-minded callousness.

Skye came downstairs.

"Hey, D," Skye said. "I ordered takeout, I didn't feel like cooking."

"Well, I suppose that will do. I didn't give you enough notice to make anything spectacular."

"Girl, you are so close to hopping back in the Bitch-mobile and getting off my property. You are so aggravating. You invited yourself over here, now you'll eat the damn Chinese food and like it."

Delva blinked in surprise. "Calm down, sister dear. Chinese is fine. Don't blow your top on my account." She paused, using her thin boned fingers to attend to a wayward false eyelash that had settled on her painted cheek. "Just out of curiosity, what are you pulling in a month from your little firm?" Lawrence gasped audibly at the very rude and very forward question. Clearly expecting an eruption of volcanic proportions, he slowly turned toward his wife.

"Delva, that's none of your damn business. I do fine for myself, and that's all you need to know." Skye exhaled, exasperated. She looked as if hot lava was about to spew from her lips. "Why the hell are you here, anyway?"

"Well, I heard through the grapevine from one of my friends that you were opening a business. I thought, gee, that's funny, doesn't she work for a consulting firm? So I gather you haven't told Mom and Dad you quit your job, huh?"

Skye propped her tightly balled fists on her hips. "No, I haven't. And I didn't tell you because you never shut your trap. What's your point, Delva?" She was in no mood to put up with Delva's mouth.

Delva smiled and slid back on the sofa, crossing her legs. "I'm sure they would be interested in this little tidbit, seeing as it's been two months and they don't even know you have this little business. Daddy will probably be very displeased that you left a good six figure job for such a gamble."

Skye moved closer to Delva and leaned down to her level. "If you want to tell them, go ahead. Otherwise, I'll tell them when I'm good and ready. I'm grown, I can do whatever the hell I want. I don't have to answer to you, or anybody else. Get the hell out of my house."

Delva rose, turning her pointy nose up in disapproval. "What kind of hostess are you? I'm your sister. You can't just throw me out. Besides, everything I've said is true, and you know it." The younger Donovan sister never went anywhere without her haughty self-righteousness.

"Delva, I'm not going to ask you again. Grab that stupid hat and get out. Enjoy your visit, but do it somewhere else. I don't want to see you again."

Delva perched the ridiculous hat back atop her head

and turned to Skye. "Fine. I don't have to stay here and eat your funky Chinese food. But now I'm telling Daddy for sure. And after he finds out what you did, I'll be the favorite, and you'll know what it's like to live in somebody's shadow!" With that, she stormed out, jumped into her yellow convertible, and sped away. Lawrence closed the door behind her and pulled Skye into his arms.

"Don't worry about her, baby, she'll get over it. Besides, what is your dad going to do, spank you?" Lawrence grinned at his wife.

"Actually, Lawrence," Skye led him to the couch, "I'd rather have you spank me."

"What about the food?" Lawrence began, but seeing the look in his wife's eyes, he knew the meal would have to wait. Lying down with arms outstretched, he beckoned to her. As Skye straddled his lap, she reached over him and flicked off the lamp.

Chapter 7
August 2005

Delva kept her promise. It was the first Saturday of August when she called her father, Louis, to tattle on her older sister. Louis answered the phone on the third ring.

"Hello?"

"Hi, Daddy, it's Delva."

"Well, hello, darling. How's my baby girl?"

"Oh, I'm just fine, Daddy," Delva drawled. "I just wanted to call you to tell you some vital information about Skye that I think you should know."

Same old Delva, still tattling on her sister, Louis mused. "So, what is it you want to tell me?"

"Skye quit her job a while ago. She's opened up some fancy pants interior design firm with Cammie. They've got a nice office, but you and I both know the statistics on small businesses. Over half of them fail within the first year."

Louis noted his daughter's snide tone. "Delva," he said sternly, "I know you're not wishing failure on your sister."

"Of course not, Daddy," she swore unconvincingly. "I was merely stating a statistical fact. I just wanted to make sure you knew about this, since Skye obviously has no intention of telling you."

"Delva, I've got to get back to my workshop. I'm working on some crown molding for one of my clients."

"Okay, Daddy. I love you."

"I love you, too, Delva," Louis answered, then disconnected the call.

*

Delva sat back on her white leather sofa, smiling

smugly to herself. "Now, let's see Skye talk her way out of this one," she said to the empty apartment around her. Satisfied she'd just made things difficult for her sister, she picked up an issue of Cosmopolitan from her glass coffee table and opened it.

*

Later that afternoon, Louis called his older daughter. Lawrence picked up the phone.

"Hello?"

"Yes, hello, Lawrence. This is Louis. Is my daughter home?"

Skye, sitting on the couch nearby, saw the way her husband's expression changed. It must be Dad.

"Yeah, hold on a second."

A moment later, Skye answered. "Hello, Dad."

"Well, hello, sunshine. How are you making out?"

"Just fine, Dad, how about you?"

"Well, I reckon I'm pretty good. What's new?"

Skye sensed the sarcasm in his voice. "I know Delva told you what I did, Dad. Let's not play games."

Louis scoffed. "Watch your tone, Missy. Yes, Delva did call and spill the beans. All I want to know is why didn't you call us and tell us?"

Skye rolled her eyes. "Dad, I was going to tell you. Actually, I planned on surprising you and Mom with a nice vacation in Miami once profits picked up. But leave it to Delva to ruin my plans."

"Skye, I'm sure you know I don't approve of you leaving such a good job for this uncertainty." His voice was taking on the 'fatherly advice' tone Skye wasn't interested in hearing.

"See, Dad, that's why I didn't tell you. You put too much pressure on me to be perfect. Now I'm finally doing what makes me happy. I knew you wouldn't agree with my decision, but I'm thirty-five years old, Dad. I don't need your permission anymore."

"Sunshine, I may not approve of what you did. But I will admit I don't know all the circumstances, and I know you're an adult now." Louis sighed. "I also know your sister only told us out of spite. She's always been jealous of you, even though we never played favorites when you were children. We love you both. I'm not calling to berate you, child. I'm calling to say you have my blessing, as well as Mary Jean's."

Skye smiled. Her father had undergone a refreshing change in attitude. "Thanks, Dad."

"So," Louis said, "when are we going to see you again?"

"Well, I may have to come up to Burlington for the fabric outlet, but I won't be able to get away from the office for a while." She paused, remembering the happy news. "Oh, guess what, Dad? Cammie is getting married!"

Louis thought for a moment. "You mean our knight with a shining bat?"

"Yeah, Dad. It's going to be on New Year's Eve. Hey, would you mind flying down here around Christmas?"

"Sounds good to me. I'll run it by your mama. Well, I'll let you go. Take care."

"You, too, Dad. Bye."

When Skye got off the phone, she went downstairs to the kitchen. Lawrence was perched on a stool at the center island, reading the sports section.

"So, how bad was it?" Lawrence lifted his eyes from the football stats.

"Actually, he said I had their blessing," Skye said, grabbing a bottle of flavored water from the fridge.

Lawrence's eyes widened in surprise.

"Hey," Skye continued, taking a sip from the bottle, "I'm just as shocked as you. But that's what he said, and I saw no need to argue."

"What are you doing today?" Lawrence asked.

"Well, I'm going to the gym first," she gestured to the purple track suit she wore, "then I've got a fitting for my bridesmaid's dress. After that, I'll probably come back home."

"Okay." Lawrence nodded. "I'm just stopping by Alan's, and then I'll be back home, too. I could use the rest with all that's going on."

"All right, baby, I'm gone. Love you." Skye leaned down and kissed Lawrence on the forehead.

"Love you, too."

Skye grabbed her lime green gym bag and her keys, and made her way out.

*

Back in Fort Lauderdale, Delva sat at her desk, spending another Saturday at the Walgreen's, where she was head pharmacy tech. It was really slow, so she had plenty of time to think about her next move with Skye. Delva paid an old high school friend of hers to leave the threatening message on Skye's machine. Knowing Skye, she would recognize the voice, but wouldn't be able to figure out who it was. Delva had also called another friend of hers, who lived in Boca, to tape that flier to the door of the office. As she sat at her desk, thinking how much fun it was to torture her older sister, she wondered what was taking so long for Pope to call her.

She was still sitting there plotting ten minutes later when the phone rang.

"Pharmacy, Delva speaking, how can I..."

"Stop reciting, Delva," a husky male voice said on the other end of the line.

"Pope. What took you so long?"

"Hey, woman, don't question me. Have you done everything I asked you to so far?"

"Yeah, baby," Delva said, smiling. "Skye is so nervous she doesn't know what to do. So, when am I going to see you again?"

Pope paused. "You know I live in Chicago. It's hard to just pick up and leave like that, love."

Delva pouted. "But I miss you. I need you." She lowered her voice into its sexiest tone. "I know you want to come and get a little taste. Besides, you run that medical practice, don't you? Just have somebody cover for you; take your patient load for a few days. You're a dermatologist. Nobody will die if you're gone awhile."

Pope thought it over. "Okay. We have to plan our next move, anyway. I'll catch the red-eye tonight and meet you at the airport in the morning. Just keep quiet about us, okay?"

"You know I will, Pope. I love you," Delva cooed, fantasizing about all the ways she would show him.

"Yeah. I'll see you about seven in the morning. Bye."

The rest of the day flew by as Delva fantasized about Pope's expert lovemaking. That night, around eight, she was driving home when she decided to make a stop at the Garden of Eden, a lingerie and adult novelty store near her apartment.

The small boutique was quiet for a Saturday night. Only three other people were in the store, one being the pale, Emo girl cashier, and the other two a young, starry-eyed Hispanic couple. They stood near the erotic books display in the back of the store, holding hands and whispering lovers' words to each other. Shaking her head at their newlywed-like behavior, Delva made her way to the rounders in the store's center section.

Browsing through the racks of risqué clothing, she finally settled on a black leather bustier set. Along the mirrored east wall of the shop, she chose black vinyl thigh boots from the shoe rack. Pausing to observe the varied and colorful assortment of toys along the west wall, she approached the counter, placing her purchases on the Formica surface.

"Can I help you?" Emo girl asked, with little enthusiasm.

"As a matter of fact, yes. I'd like one of those riding crops on the wall behind you, and some leather restraints, please." Delva flashed her very best 'good girl' smile.

"No problem." The cashier retrieved the items Delva requested from the hanging display, and added them to the pile of things she set on the counter. "Will that be all?"

"Yes." Delva handed the cashier her gold card. When everything was paid for and bagged, she nodded politely. "Thank you." On the wings of love, she floated to her car.

As she pulled out into traffic with her purchases, she smiled to herself. I can't wait until he gets here. After we make mad, passionate love, we can figure out a way to make Skye pay for being Mom and Dad's favorite, and for humiliating Pope. Delva laughed aloud as she turned into the parking lot at her apartment complex and made her way upstairs. She's going to wish she was never born.

*

The next morning, Delva was at Gate AA of Fort Lauderdale-Hollywood International Airport at six forty-five, waiting for Pope's flight to arrive. When he finally came out, she smiled brightly at him. Delva fought off the urge to drool as she surveyed the painfully good looking Dr. Maurice Gregory Pope -- his tall, muscular frame, the perfectly trimmed goatee gracing his bronzed face. She approached him, snatching off his gray fedora and adoringly raking her hand through his mass of neatly groomed twists. His hazel eyes flashed, and Delva knew his desire was building.

He looked slightly annoyed, brushed the wrinkles from his suit, and placed his hat back on his head. Surveying her, he said, "D, this is Florida in August. Why the hell are you wearing a trench coat and boots?"

As he slipped into the seat next to her, Delva kissed him deeply. "You'll see."

Back at Delva's apartment, she waited just long enough for Pope to drop his bags in the closet before she dropped her trench coat, revealing the black leather bustier set and thigh boots. Pope's eyes widened in surprise, then darkened with desire. Delva handed him the riding crop she purchased, turned away from him, and bent over.

"Do it, baby." She wriggled her narrow hips in a manner meant to be enticing.

Pope stripped off his jacket, shirt and tie, and loosened his pants. Then he obliged Delva, slapping her tight little behind with the riding crop. Each time he did, she sounded off.

"Oh!" Delva cried out at the pain that hurt so good.

Pope dropped his pants around his ankles and sat down on the edge of Delva's bed. His erection was obvious through his bikini underwear.

Delva took the hint and knelt before him, freeing his aching hardness from its tight restraint and plunging it into her mouth. Pope grabbed the back of her head, forcing himself farther down her throat. She had done this many times before over the past year, and Pope was still amazed she didn't choke. Delva moaned around the member stuffed in her mouth, and soon Pope was moaning too as he filled her mouth with his fluid.

Delva swallowed and jumped into Pope's lap, grinding against him. As soon as he was hard again, he positioned her on her hands and knees in the center of the bed. Yanking the tiny leather thong down around her knees, he pushed two of his large fingers inside her and she screamed with pleasure. He waited until she juiced all over his fingers, then thrust inside her forcefully.

"You like it?" Pope asked, as he rammed into her. He was well aware that she did, but he wanted to hear her say it.

"Yes, Pope..." Delva moaned.

"Whose ass is this?" Pope relished the control he had over her. She would follow his every command without question, and the way he was working her body right now was the key to his authority.

"Yours, baby...don't stop..."

He kept up his pace, withdrawing and pushing into her like a piston, until he felt the orgasm building. As he howled, Delva let him pull out, then turned over on her back. Pope had not yet lost his powerful erection. Pushing Delva's legs up, he put three pillows under her narrow hips.

"Baby, you gonna do me that way? From behind?"

"Yeah. Just relax, baby girl." Pope looked down at Delva as he slid into her in a new way. It was slow going, and he had to exert a lot of self-control to avoid hurting her. He knew if he hurt her now, he'd lose his minion and current 'favorite screw'. Beads of perspiration popped up on his forehead as he inched past her core. Delva whimpered beneath him. It was hard to be gentle with her narrow passage gripping him so tightly, but she would eventually relax and let him take her fully.

"I'm ready, baby," she whispered, and he let himself go, pressing himself in as deeply as possible.

They continued to make love long into the evening, and before it was over, one of Delva's neighbors called the police to check on her, thinking she was being murdered.

But Delva didn't care. Even after she sent the cops away, she was not ashamed or embarrassed in the least. All that mattered was doing whatever Pope wanted her to do...and getting even with Skye.

*

August 9th, around ten at night, Terri Kirk parked her car in the lot of her off-campus student housing building. As she locked her car and walked toward her apartment, she heard footsteps behind her. Glancing behind her, Terri saw no one. Continuing through the lot toward the stairs, she heard steps again. This time, when Terri turned around, she saw a petite female figure shrouded in darkness. Terri clutched her purse and pulled out a can of mace.

"Who are you?" she called out to the shadowy figure. "What do you want?"

The woman came close enough for Terri to hear her voice. "I want you to quit your job."

"Why? What are you talking about?" Terri stood her ground, pointing the mace at the slight woman. "If you're going to attack me, do it. I can take you."

The woman approached Terri slowly. For a brief moment, she passed under a streetlight, and Terri could make out some of her features -- the long, stringy blond hair, the NCCU letter jacket. As she came closer, Terri stood defiantly, until she realized the woman had a knife. By that time, it was too late to run.

Pointing the knife toward Terri's neck, she spoke. "If you don't quit, I will kill you."

"All right, okay..." Terri stammered . "I'll quit tomorrow. Why do you care about my job?"

"Because," the woman said, "I hate Skye Holdron. I want to make her life as difficult as she's made mine."

With that said, the woman turned and dashed into the woods behind Terri's building. Terri ran up the stairs and into her apartment to tell her roommates what just happened, and alert the police.

Chapter 8

August 2005

Friday morning, August 10th, Skye's attention was drawn from her sketches by the ringing of her desk phone. She absentmindedly grabbed the receiver.

"Hello?"

"Mrs. Holdron? It's Terri Kirk."

"Yes, dear. Aren't you supposed to be here this morning?"

"I won't be there today. I... can't come back to work."

Skye sighed. She really wished she had some advance notice so she could have called the temp agency for a replacement. "Terri, this puts me in an inconvenient situation. Would you mind telling me what happened? You sound very flustered."

"Last night, this woman stopped me in the parking lot. She had a knife... and she told me if I didn't quit... she would kill me. When I asked her why she cared about my job, she said it was because she hated you." The tremor in her voice told Skye the young woman was quite shaken by the ordeal.

Skye's face filled with worry. "I knew it. Did you call the police?"

"Yes, ma'am. The university police and the local police showed up. I gave them a description. It was dark, but when she walked under the streetlight, I saw her. She was black, light skinned and had long blond hair and dark shades. She was very petite, also. But that knife gave her an advantage, know what I mean?"

"Yes, Terri. I understand. I won't ask you to come back, at least not until you feel more comfortable. Is there anything else you can remember about her? Anything at all?"

Terri thought for a moment. "Yeah. She was wearing a burgundy Starter jacket. It said 'NCCU' in big white letters. I'll tell you, Mrs. Holdron, I won't be comfortable until that nut is in jail..."

Skye sighed. "All right, Terri. Thanks for calling." Skye hung up and walked around to the reception desk to tell Cammie what she'd just heard.

Cammie shook her head. "I just don't get it. If Pope is really behind this, he must have a girlfriend or something."

Things are getting weirder by the day, and there's no end in sight, Skye thought uneasily. "It just doesn't make sense. Sending some woman to do his dirty work? That doesn't seem like him. But no matter what happens, I know he is the root cause. You know, the woman that Terri described?"

"What about her?"

"She kind of sounds like Tamika Davis. Remember her? She went to Central, and she was Pope's girlfriend. Of course, he was too busy torturing me to pay very much attention to her."

"She was black? Wasn't she the one with that awful red dye job?"

"That's her. But if she were to put on a blond wig..."

"Oh, I get it. But how can we be sure?" Cammie sat forward in her seat. She looked excited at the prospect that she and Skye would get to play detective.

"We can't. I just have to figure out a way to get to the bottom of this mess."

"Meanwhile, how the hell are we going to finish the Massey's house if you've only got one assistant?" Cammie asked.

"Looks   like   we're   shutting   down   the   office.

Congratulations, Cammie, today will be your first day 'out in the field'."

Cammie shrank back. "Come on, Skye, I don't know anything about decorating. My knowledge doesn't go beyond this desk." She held up her hands as if to fend Skye off. "Plus, I'm gonna miss 'All My Children'," she added jokingly.

"Sorry, Cammie. We don't really have a choice. "

Cammie sighed, but relented. "It would only be temporary, after all."

Just then, their other assistant, Annette Shelton, walked in.

"Hi, Mrs. Holdron, Ms. Hamlin. Where's Terri?"

Skye walked over to the young woman. "I don't think Terri will be coming back anytime soon."

Annette frowned. "That's too bad. I liked her." She paused. "So, are we still going to do that last room at the Massey's?"

"Of course we are," Skye said. "The Masseys are major clients. They own a grocery chain in this region. We can't let them down. So until we can replace Terri, Ms. Hamlin is going to help us out. We'll just have to close down the office. Any calls will be forwarded to my cell phone, anyway." Skye grabbed her purse from the side of Cammie's desk. "Let's get going."

I can't let this anxiety ruin my business, Skye thought, as the three of them got into her truck and headed toward the Massey mansion. Deep down, she couldn't deny the strange events of the past few weeks starting to take its toll on her.

*

Sunday afternoon, Jasper and Kyoko were lounging around the house. Kyoko wore a white slip dress and furry slippers; Jasper wore a pair of red silk boxers.

Kyoko watched her husband intently as he thumbed through the pages of a European travel magazine. It was so hard to let you back in, but I'm willing to try, she reflected . Don't let me down again. As they reclined on their new bed -- the one she had insisted be replaced after his indiscretion -- Jasper turned to her.

"Ky, I love you."

Kyoko's eyes softened at Jasper's sincerity. "I love you, too, Jasper."

Like a child seeking comfort from his mother, he buried his face in the slight swell of her bosom and wrapped his arms around her. Kyoko smiled and returned his embrace. Just then, their reverie was broken by the ringing phone.

Kyoko reached to the bedside table to answer it. "Holdron residence."

"Yes, Mrs. Holdron, this is Tristan Ellis. Are you busy?"

"No, Dr. Ellis. What is it?"

"I hate to disturb you on a Sunday, but I'd like you to come into my office tomorrow. Would that be possible?"

Kyoko covered the receiver and turned to Jasper. "Is there a time we can see Dr. Ellis tomorrow?"

"I guess around six."

Kyoko spoke into the phone. "We can be there around six."

"Good, Mrs. Holdron. I'll see you tomorrow, then. Have a good evening."

Kyoko hung up the phone and turned to her husband again. "I wonder why he wants to see us."

"I don't know." Jasper settled back into the sweet smelling swell of her breasts. "I guess we'll just have to find out when we get there."

They lay there, just holding each other, for a good part of the day. Eventually, Kyoko fell asleep on his chest.

At eight, the phone rang again. This time, Jasper answered. "Hello?"

"Hey, it's Lawrence. What up, boy?"

Jasper grinned. "Hey, L. Nothing much, just holding my wife." His tone turned serious. "I don't know if I ever thanked you for helping me out, and hooking us up with Doc Ellis. I really appreciate it, man. You are one cool ass brother."

Lawrence chuckled. "Of course I am. Just don't screw up again. I may not be able to bail you out next time, and I'm not sure I'd even try."

"Don't worry, man. I've changed my ways." He looked at Kyoko, listening to her light snores ruffling the silence in the house. "I just think about how close I came to losing my soul mate, how empty life would be without her. That keeps me in check. So what are you and Skye up to today?"

"Not much, just hanging around the house. We rearranged the furniture downstairs. Hey, man, I hate to ask you this, but I just gotta know. Have you and Kyoko done it since your extreme lapse in judgment?"

Jasper sighed. "No, man. We both took all the STD tests and everything came back negative." He paused, and then continued, lowering his voice. "I haven't had any in two months. My balls are bluer than a Duke jersey. But I know I need to wait until she's ready to be with me again."

"So, what is she doing right now?"

"She's asleep."

"Wake her up! Maybe she's ready now. I'm sure she's thought about it."

"I'm getting off this call with you before you get me back in the doghouse. Goodbye, Lawrence."

"Yeah, bye, Jasper."

As Jasper reached over Kyoko to hang up the phone, she stirred. Slowly opening her eyes, she looked up and saw him. They smiled at each other, and Kyoko sat up.

"Jasper ..." she said breathlessly, stroking his naked chest.

"Yes, dear?" Jasper looked into her dark brown eyes.

"I want to make love." She held his gaze, watching for a reaction. "I'm ready to share myself with you again. I know you're not perfect, neither am I. But I love you too much to stay angry and cold." She grasped his hand and laid it on her chest. "It's OK ... You can touch me."

Jasper felt his face dampen with tears. "Baby, I'm so glad you...I love you so much. I just hope you can forgive me, trust me again."

Kyoko smiled down at him. "For now, Jasper, let's just feel our way through it, okay?"

Jasper pulled Kyoko into his arms and held her close, breathing in her scent. She smelled and felt like heaven to him. "Okay."

That night, Jasper was more passionate, more considerate, and more tender with Kyoko than ever before. She was his queen, and he put his whole heart and soul into serving her. From the time he slowly undressed her until the time she fell into an exhausted sleep in his arms, he showed his devotion in the most beautiful, carnal ways he could think of. They shared something special that night, as Kyoko realized Jasper was sincere, and Jasper realized he couldn't live without her. They were one breath, one heartbeat, one flesh, and when the Miami skyline burned with the gold, oranges, and purples of sunrise, their bodies were still intertwined.

*

The next day, when they went in to see Dr. Ellis, he asked them to perform a special communication exercise.

"What I'd like you to do," Dr. Ellis began, procuring

two pens and two sheets of paper from his desk drawer, "is write down the three most important things in your life, with one being most important. Don't show your list until I ask you to." He handed Jasper and Kyoko a piece of paper and a pen each, then returned to his seat behind his desk. "Take all the time you need."

For the next few minutes, the office was blanketed in silence as the couple worked on the assignment. When Dr. Ellis felt the appropriate amount of time had passed, he spoke again. "Okay. Kyoko, read me your list."

"I have security as number three, family as number two, and...my marriage as number one." Kyoko placed the paper on her lap and turned to Jasper expectantly.

Dr. Ellis nodded in his direction, and he revealed his list. "Three is finances, two is family, and one is my marriage." A wide grin spread over Jasper's face as he finished. "How's that, Doc?"

"Very good. Now that you both have nearly identical priorities, I'd say you're on a firm foundation. You're well on your way to reclaiming a loving and stable marriage."

Jasper turned to his wife, whose porcelain cheeks had filled with redness. He could tell she was excited. "Isn't that great news, honey?"

Kyoko gazed at him, her brown eyes sparkling with happiness. "It's the best news I've heard all day."

*

That evening, Pope drove around Fort Lauderdale in a rented black Mercedes when his cell phone rang. It was Delva.

"Baby girl. Where are you?" Pet names and fake gestures of affection were his points of leverage with Delva. Of course, she was too stupid to doubt his sincerity.

"I'm on Ninety-five, headed back into Fort

Lauderdale."

"So, did you do what I asked you to?"

"Yes, Pope. I shook up that Kirk girl last night. I'm sure she's quit her job by now."

"Delva," Pope said suddenly, "I hope you made sure nobody would recognize you. You were in the Hot Zone." I don't give a damn, except if they catch her, she'll sing like a canary.

"Nobody was in the lot except me and her. I was wearing all black, dark shades, and the blond wig. And just in case, I wore an old NCCU jacket." Delva sounded as if she were reveling in the sheer pleasure of making Skye suffer. "Your plan to frame your old girlfriend is just so...diabolical. I love you, Pope. Skye is going to pay."

"Yeah, okay. I'll see you back at your place tonight."

"I'll be there as fast as I can. I've been a bad girl, Pope. Are you going to punish me?"

She was coming on to him, and he took the bait. "Oh, yeah, D, I'm gonna punish you."

As soon as he hung up with Delva, his phone rang again.

"Hello?"

"Hello, Maurice. This is William Baxter." His partner's all-business demeanor was apparent, even over the phone.

"Dr. Baxter. Is everything all right at the practice?"

"Yes. The patients are asking for you, though. I just wanted to let you know, you picked up a new patient this week since you've been gone. I tried to refer her to Dr. Young, but she said she knew you and didn't want anyone else."

Something about Dr. Baxter's words made Pope very nervous. He raked his hand through his tightly twisted locks. I wonder why she wouldn't take an appointment with Charlene? "What is her name?"

"Tamika Davis."

Holy shit, Pope thought. She's on to me.

What were the odds that, out of the blue, an old girlfriend from college would be trying to see him now? Especially since their breakup had been so abrupt. No reason he could think of. He had a feeling this had nothing to do with Tamika's complexion.

"Well, thanks for the info, Doctor Baxter. I'll see you back at the office on Monday."

"All right, goodbye." William disconnected the call.

As Maurice headed toward Delva's apartment, he wondered. How bad has Delva really been? Has she been talking to Tamika?

*

Cammie pored over fabric samples and menus from the caterer late into Friday night. Wayne sat across from her watching television.

"Wayne, don't you have any opinions about this stuff?" She looked at him with pleading eyes, desperate for him to take some of the wedding planning pressure off her.

"Not really, Cam." He came over and kissed her on the forehead. "I just want you to have the perfect day. You deserve it." His response was honest, though it wasn't what she wanted to hear.

Cammie smiled up at the man she was going to marry. He was, after all, just a man, and thereby inherently unable to tell the difference between cranberry and scarlet. "Well, could you help me choose the menu? Please? I've still got to choose fabric for the tables at the reception, pick flowers at the florist, finish the seating chart..."

"Slow down, honey. Everything is going to fall into place. We already addressed the invitations, right?"

Her feminine obsession with the details of the wedding

was probably amusing to him. She wanted everything to be just right for their special day. At this rate, Cammie felt that if he didn't step in to help, her head would explode. "Yes, but ..."

Wayne placed a silencing finger over her pouting lips. "And we will mail them at the end of the month so everybody has plenty of notice, right?"

"Yeah, but..."

"So, as long as we have some guests and a minister, even if everything else falls through, I can still make you my wife. To me, that's all that matters, Cam. "

"Oh, Wayne." Cammie stood and embraced him. "You are so sweet." She closed her wedding planner. "Thanks for putting things in perspective."

"It's the least I can do," Wayne said, smiling. "You put up with me this long. Guess what?"

"What?" She loved his surprises. He always knew just what her heart desired.

"On Labor Day, we will be spending a romantic weekend in sunny Fort Lauderdale."

Cammie beamed. He was right on, as usual. "Wayne! Oh, that's so great! I already know the office will be closed, and I am in desperate need of a vacation. I love you!"

"I love you, too, Cam." Wayne grasped her hand and pulled her toward their bedroom. "Come on in here so we can show each other just how much."

"Wayne..." Cammie said quietly, her face flushed. "Now? I've got so much to do..."

"Shh. It can wait until morning, can't it?" Wayne unbuttoned his shirt and tossed it away, a wicked glint in his blue eyes.

"Well, I guess..." Cammie's gaze traveled the lines of his solid torso, and desire overtook her.

"Now you're talking, Cam." With that, Wayne scooped her up and carried her into the bedroom, closing the door behind them with his foot.

Chapter 9
August 2005

After Terri left, it was slow going. Finding an assistant was Skye and Cammie's top priority, because they needed the office open. Constant calls to Skye's cell phone became a major interruption to her work. Finally, on the seventeenth, they hired someone to fill Terri's position. As he walked out of Skye's office, Cammie strode in.

"So, do we have a much needed assistant now?" Cammie took her regular perch on the edge of Skye's desk.

"Yes. James Spindler, an art history major at Palm Beach County Junior College." Skye placed the paperwork he'd just given her in a manila folder marked with his name. "He brought in his transcript, and he has a three point six GPA."

"I get that he's qualified, but what's he like? Do you think he'll get along well with Annette and the other people we work with on a regular basis?"

"He has a very pleasant attitude, and I think he'll be an asset to the company. And he's just in time. We're starting on a new job next week for Councilman Manuel."

"I guess you wouldn't hire someone with an attitude." Cammie smiled, scooting off the desk's edge. "I bring enough of that to the table, right?"

"Cammie, get out of my office, nosy woman. I'm out of here. I've got an eleven-thirty flight to North Carolina."

Cammie turned in the doorway. "Oh yeah, where did you say you were going again?"

"I'm visiting the fabric outlets in Burlington, but I'm staying in Chapel Hill at this new luxury hotel called The

Franklin." Skye reached into her purse and laid a hotel business card on the desk. "I'll be in room three twenty-eight, and I should be there by nine. Call me if there's an emergency."

"Cool. Have a good trip." Cammie waved as Skye left the office, headed to the parking lot.

On the way to the airport, Skye called Lawrence.

"Hey, Skye. On your way out of here?"

"Yeah. I'm about five minutes away from my gate. I just wanted to say I love you. I'd better not come back and find the house in disarray."

"I love you, too," Lawrence said tightly. "I'll do my best, but I can't promise it will be immaculate. I'll call you later on tonight, okay? Bye."

*

After catching a power nap in the air, Skye arrived at R.D.U. International Airport around three that afternoon. She rode the shuttle to Enterprise and picked up her rental, a black, late model sport utility vehicle. She drove into the nearby town of Burlington, and spent three hours perusing a small shop called Hinshaw Yarns for fabrics. There, she placed a special order for the gold tassels and tiebacks she would need for Councilman Manuel's drapes, which would be handmade by Mrs. Hinshaw and delivered to the office.

As she left Hinshaw Yarns, she couldn't resist the urge to stop by the nearby Bridal Market. She entered the store, and was immediately enchanted. In a glass case near the counter was the loveliest assortment of bridal headpieces Skye had ever seen.

"Welcome to Bridal Market," the smiling, fair-skinned woman behind the counter began. "How may I assist you today?"

"Hi." A grinning Skye eagerly approached the counter.

"My best friend is getting married on New Year's Day, and I think I just spotted the perfect gift for her." She pointed to an especially sparkling tiara on the front row of the display. "Is that sterling silver?"

"Yes, it is," the clerk confirmed, carefully removing the delicate piece of jewelry from the case. "And those are real Swarovski crystals."

Skye could clearly see the glistening object nestled in Cammie's curls as she made her way down the aisle. "It's absolutely gorgeous. Box it up for me, please."

"Yes, ma'am."

Thrilled with her purchase, Skye left the store around six, headed to her hometown of Chapel Hill.

Cruising the tree-lined campus of the University of North Carolina, Skye reflected on the days she spent there as a child, visiting the classes her mother taught, seeing laser shows with her father at Morehead Planetarium, staying at the Carolina Inn on long weekends. She passed by the Baptist church she had attended, smiling at the memory of her wedding there back in 1993. It was hard to believe she and Lawrence had been married almost eleven years.

When Skye pulled in front of her childhood home, her mother was already on the porch. She waved as Skye made her way up the cobblestone sidewalk, recalling this house was one of few in the city never rented to students.

When Skye made it to the porch, she reached for her mother.

"Mama!" she exclaimed, as they hugged.

"Oh, Skye. My baby." Mary Jean kissed her child on the cheek, which was a stretch. "Lord have mercy, when did you get so tall?"

"Oh, Mama." Skye giggled, retrieving Cammie's package. "It hasn't been that long since you've seen me. I'm wearing stilettos."

Mary looked down at Skye's feet and shook her head. "Child, I still don't know how you walk in those things. Come inside the house. Your daddy's waiting."

Skye then followed her mother into the living room. Louis sat in his favorite armchair, watching the news.

He looked up, noticing Skye. "Hey, Sunshine, how are you?"

"Just fine, Daddy. What's new?"

"Not much of anything. Just taking it one day at a time. So, did you get what you needed up in Burlington?"

"I ordered things. I'm having them shipped to my office in Boca Raton." Skye plopped down on the sofa. Sighing, she took a long sip from the iced tea her mother handed her. "It's good to be home again. Florida's beautiful, but it's so humid down there. I miss North Carolina." Her eyes wistfully observed the tree lined street outside the picture window.

Her mom must have seen an opportunity, and took it. "Then why don't you move back home?"

"I can't, Mama. I just got my business going and I've got some pretty wealthy clients now. If I come back home, it'll have to wait until retirement."

Her mom deflated a little. She obviously missed her daughters, but didn't say anything because she didn't want to deny them the pursuit of their dreams. "I understand, baby. I'm proud of you."

The smile that brightened her face showed Skye her mother was pleased.

For a brief moment, Skye looked at her mother's caramel colored face. Seeing her disappointment, Skye decided it would be best to change the subject. "Mom, I love your haircut. It makes you look so young."

Her mother raked her hand through her short, auburn locks. "You like it? I was going for a 'Halle Berry in the early nineties' look." She gestured to her husband. "Your

92

daddy doesn't care for the color."

Louis grunted. "I like it. I just don't want those college boys flirting with my woman. She looks more like your sister than your mother now with that sassy hairdo." Smiling, he eased to his wife's side, slipping an arm around her waist. "I told her she's always been beautiful to me."

Skye laughed aloud at their play, but inside she was deeply gratified to see her parents so in love after so many years together. "Dad, how are you doing?"

"Good." Her dad released her mother, and crossed the room to kiss his daughter on the cheek. "And how have you been, sweetheart?"

"Pretty good." Skye returned her father's greeting kiss. "So, how was work today?"

"I took a day off when I heard you were stopping by." Seeing Skye's eyes resting on his 'Donovan's Home Improvement' tee shirt, he continued. "I wear these shirts most every day. Good advertisement, you know."

"What's in that pretty box?" Mom's curiosity kicked up.

"A gift for Cammie. I wanted to show it to you." Skye opened the box, pulled back the fancy printed tissue paper, and held the object up for her mother to see. "What do you think?"

"My Lord," she gushed. "It's stunning. Is that real silver?"

"That's the same question I asked the clerk, and the answer is yes."

"Well, Camilla would have to be blind and crazy not to absolutely love it." Mom kissed her forehead. "This is a very thoughtful gift, Skye. It shows what a wonderful friend you are."

"Cammie's my best friend. And trust me, with all the hard work she's been putting in, she deserves it."

"Speaking of work, I've got to get back into the kitchen. I've got dinner started."

As her mother pulled on a red and white checkered apron over her slim fitting black cotton dress, Skye's stomach rumbled. "What are you making?"

"Let's see... smothered pork chops, collard greens, black eyed peas, and cornbread. And a little peach cobbler for dessert."

Skye licked her lips. "Peach cobbler from scratch?"

Her mother laughed as she glided into the kitchen. "Is there any other kind?"

"Oh, man," Skye groaned, turning to her father. "Mom's really trying to convince me to stay, isn't she?"

"You know Mary Jean," Louis answered, "she may be an English professor by day, but by night, she's the best cook this side of the Mason-Dixon line."

*

By nightfall, everyone had filled their bellies with her mom's delicious offerings. Louis was snoring away in his easy chair when Skye rose from the comfortable old sofa.

"Well, Mama, I'm going to the hotel." She stretched widely, hoping to shake off the tranquilizing effects of her mother's cooking long enough to make the drive.

"Oh, child, I don't know why you just didn't stay with us."

"Mama, it's OK. I've got a lot on my mind. I need the time alone. I'll call you tomorrow before I leave town, okay? Love you both." Skye kissed her mother and father, being careful not to wake the sleeping bear. As she backed out of the driveway, she blew kisses at the waving figure on the porch, and inwardly thanked God for the two people who raised her so well.

Checking into the hotel, Skye greeted the night manager, who carried her bags to her room. When she glanced at his name tag, she saw that his name was Leon.

"Thanks, Leon," she said, as she walked into her room.

"No problem, miss." She closed the door as he continued down the hall.

Skye soaked in the tub for an hour that night. Lawrence called while she was reclining in the hot water, and had it not been for the ringing of her cell phone, she would have drifted to sleep in there. She spoke to him briefly. Getting out of the tub, she slipped into her long silk nightgown and fell into a heavy, deep sleep.

*

The next morning, Skye checked out of the hotel and drove into downtown Durham. She marveled at the changes that had happened since she was last there. The police cars and city buses looked different, the latter now emblazoned with advertisements for everything from car dealerships to restaurants. The bank in the center of downtown was now South Bank. Some things remained the same, though. The Book Exchange and People's Clothier's were both still open, and not much changed about the North Carolina Mutual Insurance Building.

On Main Street, Skye ran across a restaurant in the First Union Plaza. It used to be a deli called The Marketplace. Now the sign in the window read Mountain Valley Cafe. Skye decided to try the breakfast.

"Hi. Welcome to Mountain Valley Cafe. Are you eating in with us today?"

"Sure. Thanks." Skye followed her greeter to a table near the window. As she sat down and ordered a glass of water with lemon, she noted the brightly painted mountain scene on the back wall. "I love that mural. It's so cheery and welcoming."

"Thanks. We actually had someone paint that from a photograph. I'll get you that water, okay?"

Skye looked over the menu as the man disappeared behind the counter.

A young black woman with a short, stylish haircut appeared. Skye couldn't help noticing the large tattoo of a dragon on her right forearm, and her shiny black nail polish. She set a frosty glass of ice water on the table.

Skye ordered the apple pancakes. After a perfectly delicious meal, she left a large tip for the waitress and waved to the staff as she left.

What a nice place. I have to tell Mama and Daddy about it.

Within the hour, Skye was back at RDU International. She sent a quick text message to Lawrence, letting him know she'd be home around five. The terminal attendant announced the boarding of her flight as she hit the 'send' button. Switching the phone off, she showed her ticket and boarded the flight. As the plane took off, Skye gazed at the North Carolina skyline until it faded into the background.

Chapter 10
August 2005

Monday morning, when Pope entered his Chicago practice, he checked his appointments. Sure enough, Tamika's name was there in the 9:30 slot. She would be his first appointment of, and he only had ten minutes until he would have to deal with her. He grilled Delva all through the weekend, but she insisted she had not had any contact with Tamika, so there was no way she could know what they were up to. She and Delva hung out in college. So, if she doesn't know we're out to frame her, then what does she want? The questions plagued him, and the unfortunate truth was the only way to get answers was to see Tamika, and find out what she wanted.

His reverie was broken by a sharp knock on his office door. Sure enough, there was Tamika Davis, five minutes early.

She still looks fantastic, except for that hair. That's what made her such appealing arm candy back in the day.

He watched her intently as her manicured hand pushed a blond curl away from her forehead. What is it with black women getting these blonde weaves?

Tamika spoke eloquently. "Good morning. It's so wonderful to see you again, Maurice."

She looked at him the way a hungry lioness eyed an unsuspecting gazelle. Pope rolled his eyes. "You know I like to be called by my last name, Tamika. Most people wouldn't be so rude."

Tamika laughed, tossing her head. "I called you Maurice even when we dated. And we both know very well

I'm not most people."

Pope watched her face, noting her flawless skin. "Let's not play games. Why are you really here?"

Tamika looked around a room. "To be honest, Maurice, I would like to start over, you know, try again."

Pope scoffed, amazed at her ridiculousness. "Tamika, are you for real? I mean, I didn't think what we had was all that serious." She was a good lay, and always made herself available, but still, he never loved her.

Tamika's eyes darkened into a wounded look. "What do you mean, it wasn't all that serious? I gave you two years of my love and devotion, and you reduce it to...some cheap fling?"

"I don't know what delusional ideas you had, Tamika, or where they came from, but to me, it was just a casual relationship. Also, I'm seeing someone else right now, therefore..."

"Who?" Tamika demanded, standing up. "Who is this woman?"

"I don't owe you any explanations" His tone was callous and condescending.

"Tell me who she is, Maurice." Rage crept into her voice. "I'm not leaving his office until you tell me."

Pope stood behind his desk and took on a forceful tone. "Look, Ms. Davis. I'm going to have to ask you to leave my office before I have you physically removed."

Tamika turned and started to walk toward the door. When she turned to face him again, her eyes were filled with hurt and hatred.

She scowled, moving toward him again. "Fine. I won't darken your door again. But remember this, Maurice." She produced a bottle of red nail polish from her bag, and before he could protest, she splashed the thick liquid onto his white lab coat. "You're gonna get yours. A woman's heart is not to be toyed with." She turned and walked out.

On the way out, she stopped at the reception desk, a fake smile plastered across her face. "Excuse me, Miss. I just came from Dr. Pope's office. I'm a cosmetologist, and he just set up a surprise appointment for his girlfriend; would you tell me her last name so I can put her down in my date book?"

"Sure, ma'am." The receptionist waited for Tamika to pull out her date book. "It's Donovan."

Tamika's eyes flashed momentarily. "Thank you so much. You don't know how helpful you've been."

It's that damn Delva, Tamika thought, as she got into her white sedan. I should have known. As she set off toward her apartment, she knew exactly how to wipe that smug look off Pope's face.

It was obvious to Tamika the relationship she had with Pope had been way more serious to her than it had to him. It angered her now to hear him talk about what they shared as if it meant nothing.

Over the years, she dated other men, but none with the good looks and financial stability Maurice Pope offered. Had things gone her way, she'd be Mrs. Pope, but it was not to be. His wandering eye, and later his obsession with another classmate from Duke, made that impossible.

There were a lot of things Tamika could deal with.

Playing second fiddle to Skye Donovan wasn't one of them. So she'd broken it off with Maurice, but to this day, she missed the status he had afforded her.

I know he's just using Delva to get to Skye. Even in college, her former roommate Delva was pretty gullible. It was likely she had no idea what was really going on.

But Tamika planned to rectify that.

*

Lawrence paced the courtroom at the county courthouse, making eye contact with each and every juror, as well as the judge.

"We've all made stupid mistakes while driving. There are times when we may be in a hurry, or distracted by the many pressures of life. That's no excuse for driving in an unsafe manner, but we've all done it. That is why my client is not guilty of manslaughter. He is, however, guilty of reckless driving. He is ready to surrender his driver's license and vehicle license plates today, and his driving privileges revoked. But the fact remains that he does not deserve to go to prison for his mistakes. I'd like the jury to consider this young man's age, as well as his obvious remorse, before you sentence him. Remember, this will affect him for the rest of his life. One life has already been lost. Please, don't ruin another." Lawrence turned to the judge. "The defense rests."

Judge Daniel J. Mealy tapped the desk with his gavel. "This court is now in recess for deliberation."

Lawrence walked down the front steps of the courthouse, after a brief meeting with his client, when his cell phone rang.

"Hello?"

"It's Jasper."

"What's up?" Lawrence could hear the high pitch in his brother's voice; he must have some pretty exciting news.

"Are you in court?"

"No, it's okay," Lawrence replied, as he hopped into his truck. "Court is in recess. What's going on, man?"

"Lawrence, you're never going to believe this ..."

"Try me."

"Kyoko is pregnant!"

"No kidding? Jasper, that's great! When did you find out?"

"About ten minutes ago. Actually, we're at the hospital

now. She was feeling really bad, throwing up, had a constant headache, that sort of thing. I thought she had a virus or something, so I brought her to the emergency room. That's how we found out she's pregnant."

"So, are you ready to be a father?"

"Well, I am forty-two years old. It's about time I take on some responsibility, I guess. I'm excited."

"Look, I'm on my way home. If you get any more details, call me, okay?"

"Yeah, I will. Later." He hung up, shaking his head in amazement. Jasper Holdron just accepted responsibility for something. It was almost unbelievable.

By the time Lawrence got off the phone with Jasper, he was on the highway, headed home. It would still be another two hours or so before Skye got home, so he figured he would take a nap. As soon as he got there, he slipped out of his clothes and lay across the bed.

What seemed like a few minutes later, Lawrence opened his eyes to see Skye sitting on the edge of the bed, taking off her shoes.   "Hey, sleepyhead," Skye said, when she saw that he was awake. "Are you feeling OK?"

"I'm just tired. That case is finally over, though."

"The one with a kid who hit somebody with his car?"

"That's the one. I made the closing argument today." Lawrence sat up and stretched. "I'm glad, too. I don't know how much more of that I would have been able to take."

"Well, I'm just glad nothing strange happened at work today for a change," Skye said, loosening and removing the elastic holding her hair back. "I don't know how many more unpleasant surprises I can take."

Lawrence rolled toward her. "You know, you really should talk to someone about..."

Skye raised her hand, as if to ward off his next statement. "Lawrence, honey, we've been over this.

Besides, if I need to talk, I've got you." She reached out to stroke Lawrence's clean-shaven cheek, but he turned away.

"Skye, I'm only qualified to listen," he began, sitting up on the rumpled blue bedding. "I can't really offer you a solution..."

"I don't need a solution," she interrupted, moving to sit at her vanity. As she continued, she busied herself by reorganizing her jewelry box. "I'm perfectly fine."

Lawrence stood, his muscular arms folded across his chest. "Fine? Skye, you're always looking over your shoulder. Having panic attacks, passing out at work...how is that fine?"

Skye looked away from his reflection in the vanity mirror. Tears welled in her brown eyes, threatening to spill down her cheeks.

His eyes softened, the way they did when she cried. He sought to comfort her, placing his hands on her shoulders. "Look," he said softly. "I want to protect you. But even my best efforts to do that don't amount to anything if you don't deal with the root cause." He kissed the back of her neck. "You need to see a therapist, Skye."

She nodded, dabbing her tears away with an embroidered handkerchief from the vanity drawer. "Alright. But it may take me a few weeks to find someone."

"I can live with that. Just as long as you do it."

*

The following Monday, when Cammie caught sight of the office, she gasped. The place was trashed, her desk turned over, the computer screen shattered. She reached for her cell phone as she stared in disbelief.

"Police? I'd like to report a break-in at Five Magnolia

Chase. This is Camilla Hamlin. Yes, I'll be here. Thank you."

Next, she called Skye. "Skye, this is Cammie. I know it's a little early, but I think you'd better get down to the office. There's been a break-in. No— I haven't been in there. Just calm down. I've already called the police. Just get here as fast as you can."

Within minutes Skye and Lawrence arrived. She observed the police bustling about the office. One latex-gloved female officer went over the doorknob to the lobby with a short bristled brush; Skye assumed she was dusting for fingerprints. Her eyes filled with tears as she looked around the office. She and Lawrence checked the storeroom. Though it was in total disarray, nothing had been taken. Realizing no one had been into her personal office yet; she took Lawrence's hand and walked down the corridor. Through the opened door, she could see that it was in the same disheveled condition as the reception area. Lawrence must have noticed her shakiness, because he steadied her as she entered the room. The first thing she did was run to her safe, which was concealed by a reprint of one of Claude Monet's Water Lilies paintings. When she opened it, she saw that no money or documents had been taken. As she closed it and spun the combination dial, Lawrence gasped.

"What is it?"

Nervously, Lawrence grabbed Skye's shoulders and attempted to steer her towards the door. "Nothing. Let's just go back up front."

Immediately suspicious, she pulled away and walked toward her desk. "Lawrence, what are you trying to hide from me?"

"Skye, baby..."

Skye looked her desk, and saw the piece of paper Lawrence tried to conceal. He sighed, throwing his hands up in frustration as she picked it up for a closer look. It was the program from the 1991 Duke Graduation ceremonies. The large red lettering scrawled on it screamed:

I'LL BE BACK.

The program fluttered to the marble floor. That was the last thing Skye remembered.

*

When Skye opened her eyes, she was in a chair in the reception area, surrounded by paramedics. Lawrence knelt next to her, holding her hand. When he saw that her eyes were open, he sighed with relief.

"Honey, are you okay?"

"What happened?" Skye asked groggily.

"You fainted. I caught you, and Cammie called the paramedics."

"How long ago was that?"

"You've been out for about ten minutes. Are you sure you're OK?" His eyes were filled with worry.

"Yeah." Skye rubbed her aching head. "I'm OK. But I could use some painkillers for this headache."

"Miss, are you allergic to any medications?" one of the uniformed men asked her.

"No. But I have a sensitive stomach. I usually take ibuprofen for pain."

He handed her two, small, orange-coated tablets. Cammie crossed the lobby quickly, and returned moments later with a white paper cup filled with cold water. After she took the pills the paramedics gave her, she saw Annette standing nearby, and gestured to her.

"I want you to go to Stealth. It's a little spy shop downtown. Find out about their tiniest cameras and best security systems. Tomorrow, come in and tell me what you found out."

Annette nodded. "Okay, Mrs. Holdron."

"Skye, you need to stay home tomorrow," Lawrence began. "This is hard on you. You've got to rest -- and then you need to call a therapist."

Skye looked up at her husband. "No. This is my dream. I'm still in control here." She took his hand. "If it gets heavy, I promise I'll come home. But I can't just give up. I've got to prove to myself that I can get past this anxiety."

Lawrence nodded, trying to hide his frustration. He pulled her into his arms. She is too determined for her own damn good. "You are one stubborn woman." He didn't know how to make her see that she was stressing herself and their marriage unnecessarily.

They cleaned up as much as they could. Afterward, Lawrence took his exhausted and overwhelmed wife home.

Chapter 11
September 2005

Tamika looked out the bay window of the living room in her apartment. It was a cloudy Tuesday in Chicago, as humid as ever. She still seethed from her encounter with Pope the previous week. Walking away from the window, she sat on her pink chintz sofa and pulled pins from her hair.

He is such an arrogant asshole. I can't believe I ever dated him. He is so self-absorbed. He doesn't care who he hurts. He's not going to get away with it. She finished removing the pins, and her blond hair fell down around her shoulders. Miss Delva is about to get a wake-up call. And so is Maurice. I'll show him he can't treat me like yesterday's trash.

Tamika went to her computer. As she waited for her browser to launch, she smiled.

Let's do a little detective work, shall we?

An hour of tireless effort garnered Tamika what she was looking for -- an e-mail address for Delva.

"Jackpot!" Tamika opened her compose window and began to type. "Let's see if Maurice can talk his way out of this."

*

Delva was in her office at the pharmacy, logging on to the Internet. She usually surfed the Web to pass the time when business was slow.

"You've got mail," her browser announced. Opening her in-box, she saw a new message, entitled 'R U Being

Played?'" She didn't recognize the email address, but the subject line piqued her interest.

Curious, Delva opened the e-mail and read it.

Dear Miss Thing,

This is a reality check from an old friend. I know you're dating Maurice. I also know Maurice doesn't really love you. He's just using you to get your sister. If you weren't so busy getting manicures and facials, you would probably have seen that by now. So, you have to ask yourself: are you being played?

Who the hell sent me this e-mail? Pope is about to catch hell.

*

"Hello?" Pope excused himself from his patient and stood outside his office door, phone in hand.

"Pope, you have got some serious explaining to do."

"What's your problem?" Pope asked, irritated.

"I got an anonymous e-mail telling me you don't really love me, and that you're using me to get to Skye. What do you have to say for yourself?"

"Look, I don't have to explain shit. I didn't send you the stupid e-mail." Pope paced outside his office and glanced in through the glass window on the door. His patient, looking annoyed, was tapping her fingers on his desk. "And can this tirade of yours wait? I'm with a patient."

"No, Pope, it can't." Delva got huffy. "I know you didn't send it, but I know you know who did. Now you better tell me who the bitch is that did this or else."

Pope laughed. "Or else what? You're not big enough to do anything to me."He didn't care for her tone. She sounded like his mother scolding him. "I'll talk to you later."

And he hung up.

He didn't have time to listen to her bitching. Right now, he had a patient. So he closed his phone and went back into his office, a smile plastered on his face.

"Sorry about that interruption, Mrs. Wilder," he told the woman in his examination chair. "We can continue the consultation now."

*

Cammie smiled as she and Wayne walked arm in arm through their hotel, toward the lobby. It was September First, the Friday before Labor Day, and they were in Fort Lauderdale on their romantic getaway. On their way to Latin Heat, a salsa club in the heart of the city, Cammie felt incredibly sexy in the knee length red halter dress and matching stilettos she wore.

"Have I told you how sexy you look tonight?" Wayne whispered to her, as they locked the door to their hotel room. "Especially the red lipstick."

Cammie smiled. He noticed her efforts to look good for him. "I'm glad you like it." She paused, admiring his handsome profile. "I don't know how much dancing I'll be able to do, though. I'm a little tired from all the sightseeing. But I really enjoyed the Fort Lauderdale Museum of Art."

Wayne nodded. "I liked it, too. I thought it was going to be boring, but it actually wasn't that bad."

"Well, that antique car museum was a compromise, but it wasn't that bad, either." Cammie kissed his scruffy cheek. "I'm just glad none of the cars were for sale."

When they pulled up Cammie took in the scenery. The club was brightly painted in shades of yellow and orange, and a large, flashing neon sign above it had "Latin Heat" spelled out, with dancing flames as a backdrop. The night air echoed with the pulsing beat of music and the din of conversation from the line of people waiting. Cammie noticed how long the line was as Wayne stepped out of the car. Walking around to the passenger's side, he opened her door.

"Look at that line," she said, taking his hand and stepping out of the car. "If you weren't friends with Connie, we would never be able to get in here." She was referring to Consuelo, a Colombian-American woman Wayne went to high school with.

"I know. I hear it's always like this." Wayne led Cammie across the lot by the hand. "That's part of the reason we're vacationing here. I had to see what my old buddy's club was like."

Wayne gave his name, they entered the club without hassle from the bouncer. As Wayne looked around, he could see that his old friend did well for herself. He hadn't seen Consuelo in a decade, but had heard about her business.

The crowd was thick and energetic as a hive full of agitated bees. Connie has good taste, he thought, ogling the well polished glass-top bar and the six sharply dressed bartenders working behind it. Bopping his head to the lively salsa music the DJ was spinning, Wayne grasped Cammie's hand and passed the gaggle of small tables surrounding the dance floor in search of Connie. Finally spotting her, Wayne pointed her out to Cammie. "There's Connie," he yelled over the music, gesturing to the thin, well-dressed Hispanic woman holding court near the bar. "Connie!" he called out.

"Wayne! So glad you could make it," Connie said, as she hugged him. Her accent was as thick as it had been years ago. "And this must be your lovely fiancé. So nice to meet you."

Cammie shook hands with her. "Likewise. This club is great."

"Thanks, dear. This is my dream, my life's work. I wanted to create a place where the beat never dies, you know?" Connie gestured to the dance floor. "These people come from all [different] walks of life. On the dance floor, everybody's the same, and nobody has any problems. Why don't you get out there and enjoy yourselves?" She waved, smiling charismatically as she walked away.

Wayne and Cammie stepped out on the dance floor just in time to samba. By the time the song was over, her inhibitions were lost and she was simply enjoying the music. As Wayne dipped her, she noticed a familiar face in the crowd. When she stood up, she spoke into Wayne's ear.

"Hey, isn't that...Delva over there?"

"Where?" Wayne scanned the crowd, looking for her petite frame among the crowd.

"Right there." Cammie pointed. "She's wearing a blond wig."

Wayne looked again and noticed her immediately. Delva wore a sequined black dress and black stilettos. From the way she was wildly swinging her hips and waving her hands, it was obvious she was very intoxicated. Her heavy makeup, blending with sweat, ran down her face like a multicolored oil slick.

"Let me borrow that, Wayne," Cammie pulled the digital camera from his shirt pocket. Inching closer to Delva, Cammie turned the flash on and snapped her picture.

Delva appeared momentarily stunned, but after a brief pause, she went back to her wild dancing.

Cammie walked back over to Wayne, clutching the camera. She glanced back over at Delva, who was now lifting her dress and grinding pelvises with a swarthy

Hispanic man.

"We've got to get out of here."

"Why?" Wayne asked. "What's going on?"

Cammie pulled him along by the hand. "I'll explain at the hotel. Right now, we've got to skin a cat."

Cammie dragged Wayne from the club and back to the car. As he drove them back to the hotel, Cammie grabbed her cell phone from the glove compartment and called Skye.

*

"Hello?"

"Skye, it's Cammie."

"Hey, girl. How's your romantic weekend going?" Skye sat up in bed, ready for juicy details. Lawrence snored next to her.

"Guess what? I just saw Delva at the club. She was wearing a blond wig."

Skye's eyes widened. "You mean she's the one who..."

"I think so," Cammie said. "It makes perfect sense to me. Log on to your computer. I'll e-mail you a picture. Just give me a few minutes, okay? Wayne and I are crossing the parking lot, headed for our room right now."

"Sure." Skye hung up and roused Lawrence from his sleep.

"What?" Lawrence asked groggily. "Another nightmare?"

"Come downstairs to the office with me. Cammie found something out."

Skye led her husband downstairs into their home office and got online. When she opened her e-mail in-box she quickly located the photo Cammie sent.

Opening the photo file, Skye found herself face to face with Delva, staring wide-eyed, her face streaked with sweat and blue mascara.

She wore a blond wig.

Skye picked up the desk phone and called Cammie back.

"Cammie, did she see you?"

Cammie sighed. "I'm pretty sure she didn't. She looked sloppy drunk, and was too busy rubbing her ass against some Mexican guy to notice me.

"Cammie, thank you."

"Girl, please. It's no problem. Besides, if she's behind this mess, we have to nail her. Just make sure you show it to Terri. Do it tomorrow, if you can catch up with her."

"Well, her folks live in South Carolina. But she told me she wasn't going home again until Thanksgiving." Skye shook her head in disbelief. "I'll call you tomorrow, Cammie. I've got to sort this out."

Lawrence folded his arms across his chest, looking at the picture on the screen. "I can't believe that trifling sister of yours. As if you don't have enough problems without adding her to the mix."

Skye clicked the print icon, turning to him, her eyes filled with tears. "I can. She's the most hateful person I've ever known. But I didn't know until now how deep the rabbit hole went." She laid her head on his shoulder and held on to him. "I don't even need to show this to Terri. I know she did it. My own sister -- why does she hate me so much?"

Lawrence held her close. "Don't worry about it. We'll fix that black evil ass of hers."

Skye continued. "You know, Delva never had girlfriends. She was always gossiping about people and stealing their boyfriends. Nobody ever trusted her... neither did I."

Back in the bedroom, Skye found Terri's number in her phone book and called her. When Terri picked up, there was loud music and talking in the background.

"Hello?" Terri yelled.

"Yes, Terri? This is Skye Holdron. Can I talk to you for a minute? It's very important."

"Sure!" Terri said. Skye heard a door shut, and the noise in the background quieted. "So, Mrs. Holdron. It's after midnight. I thought you would be asleep."

"Usually, I would be," Skye said. "I need you to meet me tomorrow afternoon. Do you like Italian "

"I have time tomorrow." Terri paused. "Is this about getting my job back? Because, if it is, I already have another internship."

"No. I just need to ask you something. I'll meet you at Bellini around noon."

"Okay. Goodnight, Mrs. Holdron."

"Goodnight, Terri. And thank you."

Skye hung up the phone and sank into the covers, turning to Lawrence. "Goodnight, Lawrence." She inched closer to him and he wrapped his arms around her.

"Goodnight, baby," Lawrence said. Reaching over, he snapped off the lamp.

Chapter 12
September 2005

The next day, Skye was up by ten. She let Lawrence sleep while she pulled out a pair of dark denim jeans and a yellow tank top, along with her favorite white sneakers. She pulled her hair into a ponytail and secured it with a yellow plastic clip. She went downstairs to the kitchen and started to make herself something to eat, but found she didn't have much of an appetite. So she grabbed an apple from the basket on the counter and went into the living room, crashing on the couch in front of the television. She watched a few music videos, then flipped to a cable news station and watched the ticker tape go by. When Lawrence came downstairs in his boxers, yawning, he found her sitting there.

"You okay?" he asked, flopping down next to her with a glass of grapefruit juice.

"I guess." Skye fiddled with the remote. "I don't know what I'm going to say to Mom and Dad. I mean, my little sister is about to go to jail. What are they going to think?"

"To tell you the truth," Lawrence said, looking thoughtful, "I really think once they know what she did, they'll understand why she's in this situation." He rubbed her shoulder reassuringly. "You can't just let her get away with what she's done. Don't feel guilty about something she brought on herself."

"Why are we even having this conversation?" Skye asked, lying back on the couch. "We're not even sure if it was her that threatened Terri."

She was in denial, and he was on to her. Lawrence shook his head. "We haven't heard from her yet. But we both know it was Delva." He looked up at the crescent moon shaped wall clock above the television. "You'd better get to the restaurant."

Skye rose, grabbing her keys from the hook next to the door. She folded the picture and put it in her purse. Before she left, she hugged him tightly. "I love you, Lawrence. You are so good to me."

Lawrence kissed her forehead gently. "I love you, too. And I'm just returning the favor." He grinned widely. "Now go on. Hurry home, okay?"

"In that case, I'll be back as quickly as possible." The thought of his skillful loving put pep in her step as she made her way to her truck.

*

As Skye drove to the restaurant, she speculated about what was ahead. I hope we can finally resolve this mess.

When she pulled into the parking lot, Skye saw Terri's little purple VW a few spaces over and breathed a sigh of relief. Walking inside, she looked around until she spotted Terri at a table near the back. She wore blue jeans cut offs and a Marques Houston T-shirt. Skye slid into the booth and smiled at the young woman.

"Hi, Terri."

"Hi, Mrs. Holdron. How are you?"

"I've been better. There was a break-in at the office about a week ago, but nothing was stolen."

"That's weird. I don't know anything about that, if that's what you wanted to ask me," Terri said, swirling her finger in her ice water.

"No, nothing like that. I just need to ask you...if I showed you a picture of the woman who threatened you, would you be able to identify her?"

"Yes." Terri nodded. "I saw her for just a minute under the streetlight. I remember she was a petite lady, and that she was light skinned."

Skye produced the picture from her purse, unfolded it

and slid across the table. "Is this the woman?"

When Terri saw the picture, she nearly jumped right out of her seat. "That's her!"

Skye considered her reaction. "You're absolutely sure?"

"Yes! That chick threatened my life. I remember that face, and that bad wig."

"Thank you, Terri. Would you mind skipping lunch and coming with me to the police station?"

"No problem. Hey, how do you know this crazy woman? Where did you get the picture?"

Terri and Skye gathered their things and vacated the table. As they walked out of the restaurant, Skye answered, shaking her head. "She's my baby sister."

Terri's face showed her surprise. "Wow, that's a pretty raw deal."

They got into their respective cars, and Terri followed Skye to the police station.

*

About nine Sunday morning, Delva heard a knock at her door. She rose, threw on a floral silk robe and staggered sleepily through her apartment to answer it. When she opened it, she was shocked to find two uniformed police officers.

Oh shit! Did Pope turn me in?

"Are you Ms. Delva Donovan?" one of the officers asked, holding out his badge for her to see.

"Yes, I am."

"Ms. Donovan," the other officers said, producing a pair of handcuffs, "we have a warrant for your arrest." His matter-of-fact tone terrified Delva.

"What's the charge?" Delva asked, her eyes wide.

The officer answered her in a monotonous voice; she

was just another perp to him. "Assault with a deadly weapon, with intent to injure."

Delva's mouth hung open in amazement as they cuffed her and read her the Miranda rights. "I don't know what..."

"Well, ma'am, the charge is from an incident that occurred last month in Boca Raton. You'll be informed in more detail when we get to the jail."

Delva panicked and tried to wrench herself out of the handcuffs. "Jail! I can't go to jail! I'm not even dressed!" Her mind raced with a thousand disturbing thoughts of what could happen to her if she were delivered to jail in next to nothing.

"I'm sorry, ma'am. That's not our problem," one of the officers said. "They'll give you an orange jumpsuit down at the courthouse."

Defeated, Delva let the officers drag her to the patrol car. Her neighbors watched the spectacle from their open doors and windows. She was sure they were amazed to see Delva Donovan, with unkempt hair and no makeup, arrested in broad daylight. She sat in the backseat; her head hung low with the humiliation of all as the patrol car pulled away. For the first time, she asked herself, 'Was it really worth all this, just to hurt my only sister?'

When Delva arrived at the jail house, she found out a lot of things. She was informed that the young woman she attacked was able to identify her from a photograph. Confused for a moment, she suddenly remembered the bright, unexplained flash she had seen at Latin Heat on Friday night. Someone took my picture. It was stupid of me to wear that wig. I wasn't thinking. After what happened with Pope, I just wanted to escape, to be someone else for little while. Delva surmised things would be easier on her if she just admitted what she did. So she confessed. The police booked her, took her fingerprints, and she traded in her beautiful designer silk robe for an ugly orange jumpsuit. She used her one phone call to call her parents in Chapel Hill. It was the hardest thing she ever had to do.

Gripping the cold plastic receiver of the jail house payphone, she waited for someone to answer the phone. Her mother picked up.

"Hello?"

"Mama, it's me, Delva."

Her mother's voice brightened. "Hello, sweetheart. It's good to hear from you. Why do you sound so upset?"

Delva hesitated, not knowing how to break the news to her. "Mama, I have to tell you something, and I don't want you to freak out."

"Oh, my goodness, Delva. What is it? Are you in the hospital? Has something happened?"

Delva sighed heavily. "I -- in jail."

Her mother gasped, then shouted, "Jail! What in the world? How did my sweet baby girl end up in jail?"

She leaned against the concrete wall, weary with the weight of what she was about to say. "I -- well, I threatened one of Skye's assistants."

"Threatened? You can go to jail for that?"

Delva, her voice full of shame and bitterness, said, "You can if you do it with a knife."

"A knife!" Her mama freaked out. "Delva Denise Donovan. I can't believe you acted so foolishly. Your daddy and I raised you much better than that."

"I know, Mama, but let me explain –"

"There ain't nothing to explain, young lady. If you went after somebody with a knife, you're getting what you deserve. And don't be expecting your daddy and me to bail you out. You sit right there until you regain your good sense. Do you understand me, Missy?"

Delva hung her head. "Yes, ma'am."

"I'll write you in a few days. You best stay out of trouble while you're there, do you hear me?"

"Yes, ma'am." Mama was on the warpath, so at this point, there was nothing more for Delva to say.

The officer nearby tapped his watch, signaling that her time was up.

"I've gotta go, Mama. I love you."

"I love you too, silly child." And she disconnected the call.

Delva sighed and let the officer lead her down a dim, musky corridor. After they tossed her in the cell with another inmate, she had plenty of time to think about what she did, and the situation she put herself in. She sat in the corner, curled up in a ball.

I can't believe I'm sitting in jail, all because I was so determined to make Skye's life miserable. My jealousy and hatred only made it easier for Pope to use me. I've been so stupid, she thought, as hot tears cascaded down her face. My sister may never trust me again; neither will my parents.

Delva glanced at the older, much larger woman she shared a cell with. Despite her stature, she noticed the woman looked calm and non-threatening.

"Name's Ruth Ann," the large woman announced, approaching Delva. "You don't look like any hardened criminal I ever seen in here. Looks to me like you made a pretty bad mistake." She sat down on the lower bunk, placing a hand on her shoulder. "Don't worry, child, the good Lord forgives."

Delva looked up sadly. "I hope you're right."

"Of course I am." She smiled, her face glowing with kindness. "I'm too old not to be. But you need to ask Him for forgiveness. He'll answer your prayers." Ruth Ann nodded, as if she were completely sure of what she was saying.

Delva offered a small smile. Ruth Ann's large frame betrayed her true nature; she was obviously a kind person, and a woman of faith.

It's worth a shot. I've tried everything else to ease my mind.

*

That night, Jasper and Kyoko were at Hector Ramirez, a premier Mexican eatery in Miami, celebrating their impending parenthood. They were sitting at a dimly lit corner table, holding hands, enjoying a bottle of sparkling cider.

"I just want you to know how happy I am," Jasper whispered to her, leaning across the table to kiss her on the cheek. "I'm so proud you're having my child."

Kyoko's face lit up. "I'm really looking forward to motherhood. I just hope I'll be a good parent." Her eyes shone with anticipation. The joys of a new little one were soon to be hers.

"Of course you will." Jasper noticed the hum of his cell phone, vibrating on his hip. "Excuse me, Ky." He flipped his phone open and pressed it to his ear. "Hello?"

"Hey, Jasper. It's 'Auntie Skye.'"

"Hey, sis. What's up?"

"My sister is in jail," she stated flatly.

Jasper's face showed his surprise. "What? What are you talking about?"

"Remember when one of my employees was threatened, and she quit? Well, Delva was the one who threatened her. She's been in jail since this morning. Mom and Dad decided not to bail her out."

"Wow," Jasper said. "I knew she was kind of evil, but I didn't know it was that serious."

"Neither did I, until yesterday. I showed my former

120

employee a picture of Delva in a blonde wig, and she recognized her immediately. But most of the credit goes to Cammie, for taking the picture in the first place."

"Well, thanks for keeping me in the loop. Call me back if anything else interesting happens, okay?"

"We will. Oh, and tell Kyoko I said to take it easy. Later."

Jasper flipped his phone closed, turning his attention back to his wife. "That was Skye. Delva's in jail."

"Jail?" She tilted her head to one side. "What is she doing in jail?"

"Remember that night someone threatened Skye's assistant? Delva was the culprit."

"Delva did that? Wow." Kyoko shook her head in disbelief. "That's pretty serious stuff. Whatever happened to sisterly love?"

"Well," Jasper countered, "there's a thin line between sisterly love and hate, apparently. But since neither of us has a sister, I guess we wouldn't know much on that topic."

Amazed at the things they'd heard, Jasper and Kyoko went back to their meal.

Chapter 13
September 2005

As Delva sat in the dingy cell, awaiting trial, one day seemed to melt into another. Sometime during the first week of her incarceration, Ruth Ann was released. A woeful Delva watched through tear-filled eyes as her only friend walked out of the iron-barred room.

"I'll be praying for you, child," Ruth Ann called to her, as she disappeared down the corridor. "It's not too late to trust God."

Delva heard the wise words, but was too numb to respond. More days passed, and she received a letter from her parents. Opening the envelope with trembling fingers, she read it silently.

Delva,

Hello, baby. Your father and I just wanted to check in on you. We won't be able to visit, but will try to make it for your trial. We want you to get help. We'll be behind you all the way.
Love, Mommy and Daddy

For the first time since she'd been in jail, Delva felt a flicker of hope. She was so relieved her parents hadn't disowned her that she didn't realize she was crying until two large teardrops splashed onto the paper.

Days passed, dawning and fading into night. Delva paced the small cell. When she grew tired of pacing, she sat on the upper bunk, staring out the tiny, barred window. She ate little, picking at the less than appealing food they set before her each evening. At night, she lay awake, filled with remorse.

The night before she was to be tried, Delva decided it was time to take Ruth Ann's advice. Quietly, she knelt on the concrete floor next to her bunk.

"God," she whispered. "I know we haven't talked in a long time, and I know I've been very sinful. But please hear me in your infinite mercy. I feel so guilty for what I have done. I have let jealousy toward my only sister turn into hatred, I have set out to ruin her and make her miserable, all because she is successful and I feel I am not. I know I deserve to be punished; I can accept that. All I ask is that my family will forgive me. Even if I have to go to prison, I want Mama, Daddy, and Skye to know that I regret what I did." She paused, wiping at the tears that fell with a splash to the cold, hard floor. "I want to be a better person. I want to change...please, help me change. Amen."

When Delva climbed into her cot, she slept heavily, her body exhausted from crying and worrying. Morning came too soon, and she awoke feeling just as tired and drained as before. As the guards watched her shower and dress, she wondered what her future held. Once she finished, a female guard led her, in handcuffs, to a courtroom on the first floor. When she looked around at the faces in the crowd, she saw Skye, Lawrence, Jasper, and Kyoko sitting in the front row. On the second row, she saw her parents, looking solemn. If Delva had the energy, she would have tried to smile -- put on a brave face. She hadn't seen her parents since January, and she'd hoped to see them again, but not like this. She looked at the face of the young girl she had harassed, and felt more ashamed than ever. Taciturnly, she sat next to her defense attorney and looked toward the judge.

Judge Vera McRae was an imposing figure. She was a full figured black woman with a light complexion, and deep brown eyes. Her long, dark hair was pulled back tightly into a bun, and pair of gold framed glasses perched on the end of her nose. She pounded the gavel on the block to bring the court to order.

The bailiff stepped forward. "Court is now in session. This is docket number four-five-zero-D-D-D, the State of Florida versus Delva Denise Donovan."

Judge McRae addressed the prosecutor, David Bishop. "Council Bishop, what are the charges from the State?"

"The charges are assault with a deadly weapon with intent to injure, and communicating a threat."

Removing her glasses, Judge McRae turned to Delva's attorney, Victoria Harris. "Counselor, what is the plea your client wishes to enter?"

Victoria stood. "I respectfully enter a plea of not guilty by reason of mental defect, your honor."

David Bishop spoke next. "Your Honor, the state requests that Ms. Donovan be subjected to a psychiatric evaluation before her plea be accepted."

"I'll allow that," Judge McRae stated. "Ms. Donovan, it is my decision that you undergo psychiatric evaluation during the next seven days. After we have established your mental competency, or lack thereof, we will return to session and a final decision will be made. You are hereby remanded to the psychiatric ward of Boca Raton General Hospital. Court is in recess until eight AM on October fourth."

Victoria shook hands with Delva. "Should the doctors find anything amiss during your evaluation; the case could be dismissed on the grounds of mental incompetence. I'll be in contact with you." Ms. Harris left the courtroom, and a bailiff approached to remove Delva's handcuffs. As soon she was free, she immediately ran to her mother.

"Mama...I'm so sorry."

Mary Jean held her sobbing child. "Don't cry, baby. It's

OK. There is nothing you girls could ever do that would make me stop loving you."

Delva pulled away from her mother and looked toward Louis. "Daddy..."

"It's all right, child. We know you're sorry." He stepped back, then glanced in Skye's direction. "But you know you should be apologizing to your sister. Go on." Louis patted Delva on the shoulder. "She can't hold it against you forever. Her heart is too big."

Slowly, Delva approached her sister, who was talking to Kyoko. Lawrence and Jasper watched her uneasily as she neared them.

"Skye," Delva said, her voice cracking with emotion, "I can't tell you how sorry I am... I was jealous of you. You always seemed to have everything together. But that doesn't make what I did right. I just need you to know that I'm going to get help. I want to change the negative feelings I have for you, because you are my only sister. When Mama and Daddy are gone, all we'll have is each other." Delva reached out for Skye's hand, which she reluctantly extended. "I hope you can forgive me for the things I've said and done to hurt you. I want us to be sisters...real sisters."

Just then, an officer came to transport Delva to the hospital. As he led her away, she looked back at Skye with pleading eyes. Though she'd spent a great deal of time being jealous of her, Skye was still Delva's big sister, and she needed her forgiveness.

Just before the door swung shut, Skye called out to her in a tear-strained voice. "I forgive you. We'll start over... work things out."

Delva covered her mouth, and offered a watery smile. Maybe now, she could have the relationship with Skye she should have had all along.

*

After Kyoko and Jasper left the courtroom, they reported to a local women's center for her prenatal appointment. When they arrived in Dr. Sally Johnson's examination room, they sat and talked as they waited for her.

"So, honey," Kyoko said, "are you as curious as I am about the sex of our baby?"

"Definitely," Jasper said. "If there's any way Dr. Johnson could tell us today, I'd be thrilled to know what's inside your little tummy pop." He patted her belly lovingly.

A few moments later, Dr. Johnson entered the office. Kyoko felt very comfortable with the petite, bubbly brunette doctor. Her bright smile greeted them even before her friendly words.

"Well, hello there," she said cheerfully, sitting on a stool next to the sink. "How is our mommy feeling today?"

"I feel OK. I just have a slight headache. But the morning sickness seems to be gone." Kyoko lay back on the examination table. "How about you, Doc?"

"Oh, I'm well." She stood next to the table and flipped on the monitor of the sonogram machine. "You're about twenty weeks along now. So, let's have a look at the baby, okay?"

As Dr. Johnson spread the cold jelly over Kyoko's slightly protruding tummy, Jasper raised his hand.

"Yes, Mr. Holdron?" Dr. Johnson responded. Her grin suggested she was amused by his grade-school attempt to get her attention.

Like most men, he was unsure of how to behave in an obstetrics office. "Is it too soon to tell the sex of the baby?"

"I think we should be able to determine the baby's sex

today, if the baby is willing to cooperate and let me see." She ran the hand-held device over Kyoko's belly, and a picture appeared on the screen. They watched as the baby sucked its thumb and made faces at them.

Kyoko's heart swelled as she watched Jasper look on in amazement at his first child. Just then, Dr. Johnson made a sound of discovery.

"Well, looks like you two are going to have a bouncing baby girl," she said, smiling. "She looks very healthy and strong; well-developed. Everything is going well, but Mrs. Holdron, you're going to have to put on some weight so your little princess can grow, okay?"

Kyoko nodded pensively. While she wasn't thrilled about gaining weight, she knew it would be for a good cause: the baby's health.

Dr. Johnson continued. "I'm going to give you a special diet, telling you the kinds of foods you should eat and how much to consume. You need to gain about twenty more pounds in the next ten to twelve weeks." Dr. Johnson wiped the jelly from Kyoko's stomach and removed her gloves. "Well, we're finished here, if you don't have any more questions." She walked toward the door. "I'll go get you a copy of that diet, and I'll be right back."

After she left, Kyoko pulled her blouse down and looked up at Jasper. Her eyes were filling with tears of joy. "A girl. I'm so excited!"

Jasper helped her stand up and hugged her. "Me too, Ky." He looked forward to welcoming this little bundle of sunshine into their lives.

Once they received a copy of the diet, Jasper took his wife home. There, he massaged her feet and let her recline in bed. Kyoko asked Jasper to run downstairs and bring her some pretzels from the kitchen. By the time he returned, she was fast asleep. Jasper smiled, covering her with a down throw. Then, he crept downstairs.

*

Delva underwent her psychiatric evaluation two days later. Her eyes were tired from looking at inkblots and filling out questionnaires; her throat was dry from all the talking she'd done. She went into an examination room when Dr. William E. Skidmore sat with her test results. Dr. Skidmore was a tall, Caucasian man, with a wide frame and piercing gray eyes. He wore a white shirt, red tie, and gray slacks under his lab coat. Delva was with him all day, and he was very understanding and sympathetic as he listened to her.

"Delva," Dr. Skidmore began. "My findings indicate that you may have bipolar disorder II, and that you have a problem with acute stress. Now, we can give you medication for the bipolar disorder, and we will. But your reaction to stress can only be treated through long-term psychotherapy. You need to work through your issues of jealousy toward your sister, and the feelings of animosity with it." He patted her shoulder. "I'm going to keep you here in the hospital, under my care, for about four weeks. This will allow you to get stabilized on your medication, lithium."

"Thank you, Doctor," Delva said. Whoa. This bipolar disorder sounds really serious. "You know, I have days when I'm so energetic, I get up and clean my whole apartment. And then, there are days when I feel so sad, I can't even get out of bed. I'm so glad it has a name, and it's treatable."

She watched Dr. Skidmore leave the room. On his way down the hall, he gestured to Victoria, in the waiting area. She walked over to where Delva sat. She was amazed how regal Victoria looked today. She sat next to Delva.

"I had a feeling they would find something." Victoria

looked at Delva with optimism in her eyes. "Now, Florida law dictates that you not be imprisoned. Most likely, all you have to do is agree to undergo the psychotherapy you need, and stay on your medication. Can you agree to do those things?"

Delva nodded. "I'll do whatever they say. I'm not about to go back to jail. And the doctor was right. In time, all these issues with my family can be worked through, and I can go on with my life."

"Well, now that you've been evaluated, I think we'll be able to convince the judge you should be treated, not punished. Your hearing is three days away; I'll stand in for you."

Delva thanked Victoria and watched her leave. As Victoria walked out, a nurse walked in.

"Miss Donovan," she said kindly, "I'm going to escort you back to your room and give you your first dose of lithium, okay?"

Delva stood, nodding. Finally, all the feelings she'd been having for so long made sense. For the first time in a long time, she felt at peace.

Later that day, Delva dialed Skye's number, but got no answer, so she left a voice mail.

"Skye, I wanted to tell you Pope is behind all this. I told the police but it could take a while for charges to be filed, because I don't have much proof of his involvement. Just be careful, Skye."

Chapter 14
October 2005

As the Chicago breeze whipped at the lunch crowd passing by Pope Dermatology Associates, Pope rapped firmly on the office door of his partner, William Baxter.

"Come in," William called from the other side of the frosted glass.

Pope stepped inside, closing the door behind him. "Ah, Maurice. What can I do for you?"

"Will, would you please take my patient load for this week? I have urgent business I need to attend to."

William looked up from his charts, curiosity in his eyes. "Sure. I'm light on appointments this week. Is this something you want to talk about?"

Pope paced the floor in front of the desk. "No."

William shrugged. "Let me know if there's anything else I can do."

"Thanks." Pope left.

*

Later that afternoon, Pope looked around his Chicago home to make sure he had everything needed for the long trip ahead. He gathered a few days' worth of clothes into a black duffel and put them in the trunk of his black SUV. His destination -- sunny Florida. Soon, he enjoyed the solitude of the open road. He mentally reviewed his plans as he cruised toward I-95, and the vengeance he sought.

They'll regret ever crossing me.

By the time Pope crossed the Florida state line, twelve hours passed. It took another hour and a half to get to Fort

Lauderdale. As he drove to Delva's apartment building, he didn't Delva's convertible in the parking lot. So he passed the complex and drove to the nearby drugstore where Delva worked. Hopping out for the first time in several hours, he dashed into the store and followed the signs to the restroom.

Pope approached the pharmacy pickup window. A white coated pharmacist, with wire-rimmed glass perched on the end of his pale nose, appeared.

"Can I help you?"

"I'm here to see Delva," Pope huffed, looking past the man. "Is she in today?"

"I'm sorry," the white coated man replied. "Delva no longer works here."

Pope frowned. I need more information, but how can I get it out of Pharmacist Bob here?

Without missing a beat, he said, "I'm her brother. She called me last week, and told me I could meet her here." He put on his best confused face. "What's happened?"

The pharmacist hesitated, then lowered his voice. "To be honest, she was arrested about ten days ago, and that's grounds for immediate expulsion."

Pope didn't stick around to hear the rest. He sprinted down the shelf-lined corridor toward his truck.

Pope began to sweat as he I-95 toward Boca Raton. I know she turned me in. I just know it. I made her angry, and now she's going to turn me in. In traffic on Main Street, Lawrence passed him. As soon as Pope saw his face, his heart began to pound in his ears. There's that fool. If it weren't for him, Skye would be my wife now. Pope pressed down hard on the gas pedal, swerving to change lanes, and follow the blue pickup truck Lawrence drove. He ignored the furious horn-honking of the drivers he cut off, his mind set on revenge. That's it, jackass. Lead the way to Skye.

*

Lawrence was on South Main Street when he looked in his rear-view and saw a black SUV following him. As Lawrence made a right on Deer Street, he saw the driver. Just as Lawrence made his second right on Myron Avenue, he saw a familiar face glaring at him.

"Pope! That son of a bitch is following me!" Angered, Lawrence decided it was time to settle this. He drove to Barham Park, Pope right behind him the whole way. "He isn't even trying to hide he's following me."

Lawrence parked, he took off his sport coat and loosened his tie. Cracking his knuckles, he opened the door and stepped out. Pope pulled next to him and jumped out, eyes blazing. There was about four feet of air and opportunity between them when Pope opened his mouth.

"Well, well, well." Pope started, pacing back and forth. "If it isn't Mr. Big Shot Lawyer, living high on the hog." He spat on the ground, as if it were some show of strength. "I came here looking for Skye and Delva. Who knew I'd run into your uppity ass."

Lawrence glared at Pope. "If you think you're coming anywhere near Delva, or my wife, you're stupider than you look. And if you have a problem, let's solve it right here." Lawrence stepped closer to Pope, making his intentions clear. He wasn't about to let this fool cause his wife any more anguish.

Pope scoffed. "You're not going to fight me. You're too scared to get that damned suit dirty. Besides, you know I'd whip your ass." His haughty smile and overconfident stance only served to further infuriate his former classmate.

Lawrence took another step forward. I don't back down to anybody, especially punks like you, who try to overpower a woman because they're too scared to step to a man." He stepped up yet again, and laughed in Pope's face. "I can't believe all these years passed, and you're still whining because Skye didn't want you. You're pathetic."

A breeze rustled the trees above them as Pope inched closer to Lawrence. "Look. Deep down, she wanted me. You were just a distraction. Shame she married you. She's meant to be with me." He pointed a finger in Lawrence's face. "You've always been second best to me."

Lawrence slapped Pope's finger away. "I'm done talking. Either get the hell out of town, or I'm going to splatter your ass all over this park." He grabbed Pope's shirtfront and, with very little effort, lifted him off the ground. "Don't come here, following me, trying to break bad with me unless you want your face rearranged." He shook Pope violently, then dropped him to the ground like a sack of trash. "I didn't forget you tried to rape my wife." Lawrence quickly rolled up the crisp white sleeves of his dress shirt. If Pope wanted to play with fire, he better be ready for burns.

Pope smiled. "I haven't either. If it wasn't for that white girl, I would have finished the job. So don't bitch at me. I did four years in the clink for it. If it wasn't for my parents taking care of my record, my life would have been ruined."

Lawrence scoffed, "That's so like you. Having mommy and daddy use their money to fix your problems."

"Whatever. I did what needed to get it together, and you can't stop me from reclaiming what's mine." He continued to grin, mocking him.

Lawrence growled with rage and threw Pope to the dirt. He dropped down, pressing his knee into Pope's chest. Ignoring the terrified look on his face, he hit him with a right hook, and relished the feeling of his jaw shattering beneath his assault. As he raised his fist for another blow, the sound of an approaching car made

Lawrence pause. A Park Ranger appeared, looking at them strangely.

"What's the problem here, gentlemen?"

Lawrence answered. "No problem, officer. This man attacked me and I defended myself." Lawrence rose, and Pope gave an audible sigh of relief. "I don't think he'll be so quick to assault someone ever again." He emphasized the last few words.

The ranger nodded. "That may be so. But since I didn't witness the incident, I'll have to issue you both a warning."

"I understand, sir," Lawrence agreed.

Pope did not share Lawrence's acceptance. He pulled himself to stand, and cursed. "No way. Pretty boy should be glad I didn't kill him."

Lawrence shook his head. Has he really hit Pope so hard he forgot he was losing this fight?

Staggering toward the ranger, Pope swung out with his fist, but missed his target.

The ranger frowned. "I see we've got a troublemaker." Pulling the radio from his belt, he spoke into it. "Send an officer over to Barham Park. A misguided man just assaulted me."

A short time later, a Boca Raton police officer drove into the clearing. Getting out of his cruiser, he looked to the ranger, who gestured to Pope. Grim faced, the officer got his handcuffs out and grabbed Pope's wrists.

As he cuffed Pope, Lawrence leaned close to his old nemesis and spoke softly into his ear. "If you ever come near me, my wife, or anybody we know ever again, I will kill you."

Pope shook with anger and humiliation. "He threatened me! Are you going to let him threaten me?" He tried his best to wrench away from the Ranger, but was unsuccessful. "Arrest him, too! He's communicating threats!"

Lawrence got back into his truck, watching a livid, cursing Pope forced into the back of the Ranger's nearby vehicle. Laughing , he drove away.

*

An exhausted Pope arrived at the Main Detention Center, West Palm Beach. After he was fingerprinted, photographed, and handcuffed by a large, burly officer named Evans, he was seated on a rickety wooden bench, angrier than ever. "Can I please get my phone call now?" he asked, through gritted teeth.

"Hey, buddy," Evans countered. "You better check that attitude. Nobody told you to break the law." He shook his head. "No need to sit here, pouting like a spoiled kid." He yanked Pope up from his seat. "Come on."

Evans roughly escorted the red-faced Pope to the pay phone just outside the cell block. Releasing Pope's wrists from the handcuffs, he folded his arms and stood a breath away.

Grunting, Pope snatched the receiver up and punched in the number to his parent's home outside of Chicago. Placing the phone to his ear, he listened for several rings, until the phone was answered by Mrs. Cuddy, the upstairs maid.

"Pope residence, Mrs. Cuddy speaking. May I help you?"

"Mrs. Cuddy, it's me," Pope began breathlessly. "Is my mother home?"

"Yes, sir, Mr. Pope. I'll fetch her presently."

Pope drummed his fingers on the top of the phone as he waited. Moments later, his mother's irritated voice came on the line. "Maurice? What on earth do you want now?"

"Hi, Mom. How are you..."

Delores cut her son off. "I was in the middle of a massage. Why don't we dispense with the pleasantries and you can tell me why you're calling me."

"Well, I ran into a little trouble, and I need bail money. It wasn't really my fault..."

"Of course it wasn't," Delores quipped with sarcasm, "but I don't have time to debate with you about it, so how much do you need?"

"Fifteen thousand." He sighed, preparing for the inevitable onslaught.

"You know, your lack of good sense is costing your father and me. I'll send my sister Renee with your bail tomorrow. Let's be very clear. If you ever, ever, end up in jail again, don't bother calling."

Click.

Pope looked at the now dead phone. His mother had hung up on him.

Evans took the receiver from Pope, replacing it in the cradle. "Time's up. Let's get a move on. We've got a nice room reserved for you, Mr. Pope."

The last statement was tinged with a sarcasm Pope didn't care for. Nevertheless, he had no choice but to allow Evans to re-cuff him, and force him down the hallway, his nightstick in Pope's back like a blunt ended cattle prod.

At the end of the cell block, he tossed Pope into a drab, empty cell. "Since you're so ornery, looks like you'll be in this deluxe suite all by yourself, Mr. Pope," Evans remarked, his tone snide, as he strode away.

Frustrated, Pope sank down onto the bottom bunk of the rusted steel frame bed. He knew he'd have to sit there overnight, waiting on his bail money to come. He knew his mother was angry she'd been inconvenienced again, but he couldn't stand sitting in that dingy cell any longer. Valuable time passed, moments he could be using to get closer to Skye.

That damn Lawrence, Pope thought, angrily kicking the wall next to his bunk, if he weren't around to get in my way, I could have gotten to her by now.

Then and there, Maurice Pope decided to spend his night in jail doing something useful: plotting his next move. *Lawrence may think I'm afraid of him, but he's wrong. I won't be put off that easily.*

*

The next morning, Pope's Aunt Renee came, bail money in hand. His mother's older sister was looking just as constipated as ever, he noted, as she produced a check from her handbag. She paid his fine and walked with Pope outside to her car.

"You know," Renee began, "this is the second time your parents had to retrieve you from jail, Maurice. They told me to tell you they won't do it again." The sour look on her aging face made her appear even older and more wrinkled than she actually was.

Pope rolled his eyes. His parents said the same thing back in ninety-three, when he'd gotten out of jail the first time. "I know, Aunt Renee. Don't worry," he said, his brown eyes turning cold. "I have no intention of ever going back."

*

Delva placed a folded throw into her pink leather suitcase, zipped it closed, and sighed audibly. Outside her seventh floor hospital room window, the October sun shone, and Delva was cautious and excited about getting back to real life. Sitting next to her lone suitcase on the bed, she clasped her hands and waited.

When her nurse, Kaye, arrived a few minutes later, Delva stood. Kaye passed a brown paper bag to Delva. "This is a three month supply of your medication. Dr. Skidmore spoke with you already, right?"

"Early this morning."

Sliding a clipboard from underneath her arm, she flipped through the pages attached to it. "Well, he's already signed your discharge form, so all I need you to do is sign here, signifying that you understand the instructions he gave you." Kaye presented the clipboard and attached pen to Delva, and waited as she signed her name on the signature line. Tearing off a carbon of the page she signed, Kaye gave it to her. "Ms. Donovan, you're free to go."

"Thank you." As she folded the page and placed it into her handbag, she left the room. With a new sense of hope in her heart, she left the hospital via the main entrance and was ecstatic to see her mother's black sedan idling in the pickup lane.

"Hi, baby." She rushed to her daughter, arms open wide. Delva was soon enveloped in her mother's embrace.

"Hi, Mommy. Let's go. I'm ready to get on with my new life."

She smiled brightly. "I'm glad to hear it. Your father's waiting for us."

The two women got into her car, and she pulled away from the curb.

*

It was a crystal clear, brisk October evening. Skye and Lawrence enjoyed a dinner cruise to celebrate their eleventh wedding anniversary.

Skye stood near the railing of the SS Hearts Aflame,

looking over the cerulean surface of the Atlantic. The long, flowing white satin dress and matching wrap she chose for the occasion caught the breeze, fluttering around her like a low floating cloud.

Only six couples per voyage were allowed aboard the vessel, which left from a port at Palm Beach. Lawrence had the foresight to book their spot in early spring to ensure they would be among the passengers on their special night. She marveled at the beauty of the ocean, and the starlit sky it reflected, when she sensed Lawrence behind her, breaking her reverie.

"I brought us champagne," he said softly, producing two filled flutes from behind his back with a flourish. "Are you ready to eat? The chef is sending out the first course."

He was so handsome in his white suit and crisp red shirt. The silver tie he'd chosen added a refreshing pop of color.

"Sure, honey." Taking her glass, she followed her husband to a candlelit table near the bow of the ship. "Wow, everything looks just beautiful." She admired the etched crystal goblets and fine, gold-rimmed china set out on the white tablecloth.

Lawrence smiled with self-satisfaction. "I'm glad you like it, my dear. This is the best table on the boat."

A white-coated waiter approached the table, silver tray in hand. "Good evening, Madam, Sir. Here is this evening's first course: petite Quiche Lorraine. Please do enjoy." The waiter and his French accent were soon gone.

Taking a bite of one of the tiny pastries, Skye groaned with delight. "Oh, these are heavenly. I can't wait to see what the main course is."

"Well, you'll have to wait," Lawrence countered, "because it's a surprise. Don't worry; I'm sure you'll enjoy it."

The mischievous sparkle in his brown eyes told Skye

her husband spoke about more than just the cuisine.

The two lovers enjoyed a fantastic meal of succulent lobster tails, fresh, colorful salad, and hearty clam chowder, capped off with a decadent dessert of five layer devil's food cake with chocolate filling.

As the waiter cleared the dishes, Lawrence pushed away from the table with a satisfied sigh. "Oh, man. That was some meal."

"Yeah," Skye agreed, wiping chocolate sauce from her lips.

"Come on, let's dance."

"To what? There's no music."

"Ah, but there is," Lawrence said, clapping his hands sharply.

Two-white coated men appeared, one carrying a violin, and one with a saxophone. "Any requests, sir?" the violinist asked.

"Yes." Lawrence stood, taking Skye's hand with a suave smile. Escorting her to a spot near the ship's railing, he continued, "Moonlight Serenade, please."

As the music began, Skye could feel tears fill her eyes. Moonlight Serenade was the song they danced to at their wedding. "Lawrence, this is so sweet."

"I knew you'd like it. But it gets better."

"Really?" Skye looked up into his mesmerizing cocoa eyes.

"Yes. We'll be spending the weekend at the lovely Fontaine Hotel. I'm going to make sure you never forget this day." Lawrence winked. "Meanwhile, I suggest you take Monday off. You're going to need some recovery time."

Skye blushed, and Lawrence laughed.

But before night had fallen on Saturday, Skye sent Cammie a text message; she would indeed be taking Monday off. Lawrence was wearing her out, and she loved every minute of it.

*

On Friday, November 4, Skye, Delva, Kyoko, and a host of Cammie's friends surprised her with a bridal shower at the country club. They rented the Grand Ballroom and decorated it in Cammie's wedding colors -- royal blue and sky blue. When Skye led the blindfolded Cammie into the room, everyone jumped up and yelled, "Surprise!"

Snatching off the blindfold, Cammie's eyes widened as she looked around at all the beautiful decorations, and all the friends who gathered there.

"Your mother and I planned this a few months ago." Skye patted her shoulder. "We wanted it to be a very special day for you."

"You guys -- this is too much." Her voice thickened with emotion. Everything was perfectly coordinated, from the flowers to the balloons, to the table stacked high with gifts, all wrapped in shades of blue. "Thank you so much." As she wiped at her eyes, Skye led her to an area with a semicircle of chairs, and instructed her to sit in the throne-like one at the center of them. After she sat down and accepted her glass of champagne, her friends one by one, described the Cammie's impact on their lives.

Tara, a friend of Cammie's since childhood, went first. A host of cousins, former coworkers, and acquaintances followed. By the time Skye stood to make her toast, there wasn't a dry eye among them.

"I've known Cammie for fifteen years," Skye began. "Not to give away our advanced age. She is the sweetest person I've ever known, and the best friend I've ever had. You know, she wouldn't tell you this, but she's a hero. She once saved me from an unspeakable horror, armed with only her courage and a baseball bat." Skye held back tears as she recalled Cammie's heroism. "I know she and Wayne will be ridiculously happy. Here's to Cammie." She raised her glass. "May she and Wayne always be blessed with good sex, good communication, and good kids." A cheer went up from the group of women as Skye and Cammie shared a hug.

For the next three hours, they ate, drank, and "acted a fool." When Cammie opened her gifts, she discovered it would be years before she'd need to purchase lingerie. She knew Wayne would be pleased with her new trousseau. Her gift from Skye drew a round of giggles from the women present; it was a huge purple vibrator.

Skye feigned innocence. "You'll need a little something in case Wayne is ever out of town. Although, you can use it with him..." Her voice trailed off as she winked suggestively.

"Skye!" Cammie's face was totally red.

Delva gave her a lovely red silk gown. As she handed it to her, she apologized for her shaky hands. "It's my medication. I feel a lot better, but I could do without the constant hand tremors."

Cammie held up the flowing garment. A chorus of 'oohs' and 'aahs" came from her girlfriends.

It was after dark when the party finally broke up. Delva, Skye, and Cammie were walking out of the building together, with Kyoko and Annette close behind.

"I can't thank you enough for this," Cammie said, as they stepped out into the crisp night air. "I really appreciate it."

"Don't mention it," Skye said. "Seriously, don't mention it to anyone, or all our friends are gonna be hitting me up for a vibrator."

Cammie guffawed. "You are completely ridiculous."

Kyoko chimed in. "Hey, you only get married once. We hope."

They were standing on the sidewalk, laughing and

talking, when out of the corner of her eye, Skye noticed movement in the bushes to the left of them. She tensed, but then the rustling stopped. Just as she was about to shrug it off, she saw a face in the darkness.

"Oh My God!" she screamed.

It was all she had a chance to say.

Chapter 15
November 2005

As panic swept over the group, three gunshots echoed in the darkness.

Skye cringed, gasped.

Before anyone could reach her, Skye was prone on the pavement, blood pouring from her lower abdomen.

In an instant, Kyoko was knocked to her knees, clutching her upper left arm.

Blood trickled down her fingertips.

Cammie dropped to the pavement next to them and quickly began barking out orders.

"Annette, call 911! We need the police and an ambulance. I'll call Lawrence and Jasper. Delva, let me borrow your sweater." She was in emergency mode and she knew no one would dispute her.

Delva, eyes wide with fear, took off the pink sweater she wore and handed it to Cammie, who threw it over the now shivering Skye, hoping to shield her from the chilly wind. Terri came running when she heard the shots, ripped off the bottom of her t-shirt and wrapped it around Kyoko's arm. It did little to stop the profuse bleeding, but it was all she had to offer.

Within minutes, the parking lot swarmed with country club staff, police, and emergency workers. Delva knelt next to her sister, looking into the woods surrounding the club. "I can't believe him." Turning to Cammie and Terri, she purged her soul. "This is partly my fault." She lowered her head in shame. "I had no idea he'd go this far, I swear." Cammie's eyes softened when she saw Delva's remorse. "Skye told us everything. We know you didn't mean it to go this far." She touched Delva's shoulder. "Just be here for your sister now. You can't go back and do it over."

As paramedics approached the spot where Skye lay, Cammie frantically dialed Lawrence's cell. "Lawrence, this is Cammie. You've got to get over to the community hospital."

"Why?" Lawrence asked. "What's going on?"

"We were leaving the country club, and Skye and Kyoko were shot! Just get to the community hospital as fast as you can!"

Lawrence's breath caught. "I'll call Jasper and we'll meet you there."

Cammie watched the emergency workers as they placed Skye on a stretcher, and then load her and Kyoko into the back of a waiting ambulance. She approached a nearby police officer. "Excuse me, sir, but could you follow us to the hospital? I have a feeling we know who did this and he's still out there. We need protection."

The officer nodded, assuring her. "We'll be right behind you."

When they arrived at Boca Raton Community Hospital, Lawrence and Jasper were just arriving. They joined the group of women standing just inside the automatic doors.

"Jasper, Terri, and Annette, you go and check Kyoko," Cammie said. "Delva, Lawrence and I will check on Skye. If there's news on either of them, pick up your cell phones and dial like hell." She turned and entered the hospital, too nervous and worried to wait for a reply.

The group continued inside to the triage desk, where a nurse met them.

"Those of you looking for the black lady go to the double doors and follow the signs to the intensive care unit. The rest of you can come through this office, and follow me. The other woman is with Dr. Wade right now."

The group separated. Cammie and Delva sprinted after Lawrence down the corridor. When they found Skye, she was a pitiful sight. She was awake, but surrounded by doctors and nurses, who were inserting all manner of tubes and needles into her. Lawrence broke through the medical team, pushing them aside until he was touching her frail and clammy hand.

"Sir, you have to wait --" a dark-haired nurse in lime green scrubs started to say.

"Like hell. That's my wife!" Skye saw Lawrence standing beside the gurney. He gripped her hand tightly. "Baby -- I'm so sorry I couldn't protect --"

A uniformed security guard approached. "Sir, I'll have to ask you to step back."

Lawrence complied, his anger apparent.

Skye smiled weakly. "Lawrence, you can't protect me from everything. This isn't your fault. I love you." She coughed.

Lawrence wanted to kiss away her pain. "I'll be here when you wake up." Here she was, hanging on the edge of life, and he couldn't even touch her. If she died, he swore he'd sue the hospital right out of business.

Comforted by his words, she smiled.

A tall, dark-skinned and bespectacled man in a lab coat appeared next to him.

"Mr. Holdron? I'm Dr. Fred Lee. I'm an internist."

"Yes, Dr. Lee. How is my wife?" Lawrence's face was filled with concern.

"She was shot twice in the abdomen. She needs some minor surgery, during which we'll remove the bullets, and make repairs to her small intestine and possibly her uterus. It should take anywhere from two to four hours. She should be fine. Her injuries are not life threatening."

He shook Lawrence's hand. "We're prepping her for surgery right away. Don't worry, we promise to take good care of her." The doctor looked sympathetic, Lawrence noted.

A nurse placed a mask over Skye's nose and mouth, dispensing general anesthesia. Delva stepped out of the doorway to allow an official looking man to enter the room.

He walked to Lawrence, producing a badge. "My name is Detective Thomas Devack. A woman at the scene asked me to follow you here."

Skye's attempts at speaking were finally successful. "Pope is..." she said, barely above a whisper. The anesthesia was beginning to take effect.

Detective Devack turned to Cammie, who held her blue Dell laptop. "I'll do a search on him, see if I can pull up his picture. I've got wireless Internet."

Cammie sat down, booted up the laptop, and went to work. "Aha. Here's the dermatology practice website." She turned the computer around for the detective to see.

Detective Devack leaned over to get a better view as she pointed to the color photo.

Cammie explained,"This is him. Skye must have seen him before the shots were fired."

"Miss," Detective Devack said, leaning over a very drowsy Skye. "Are you absolutely sure this is the person who fired the shots at you?" He gestured to the photo.

"Yes ..." Skye mumbled, drifting to sleep. "Saw him ... in the bushes ..."

Detective Devack nodded. "Okay, folks, I've got to get back to the station and do some checking on this Pope character. Take care of her. We'll need to get a statement from her when she's ready." He jotted Pope's name onto a notepad, then replaced it into his front inside jacket pocket.

"Thank you," Delva said, as he made his exit. Dr. Lee and his nurses re-entered the room shortly after he left.

"We need to get her to surgery, sir." Dr. Lee smiled reassuringly. "We'll have her back to you as soon as possible."

Lawrence kissed Skye's cheek and watched mournfully as they wheeled her away. Cammie came over and hugged Lawrence for the first time since they'd known each other.

"Don't worry about Skye, she's a fighter," Cammie said. "It takes more than a jackass like Pope to hold her down."

The group made their way to the ER waiting area. They filled the few available seats, and waited for what had to be the longest three hours ever.

*

Downstairs in the emergency room, Jasper, Terri, and Annette were watching over Kyoko. She was reclining on an examination table, her face contorted with pain. Dr. Erica Wade was next to her, using a pair of tweezers to remove the bullet from her upper arm. Jasper's cell phone vibrated on his hip. When he answered, Delva filled him in on Skye's condition.

"Skye is in surgery," Jasper told the others, as he flipped his phone closed. "They're going to do some repair work on her small intestine and uterus, but the doctor says she'll be fine." He directed his attention back to his wife. "Is she still going to be able to use this arm?" he asked the doctor.

"Yes," Dr. Wade said, as she dropped a bloody bullet into a metal tray. "But she will need to wear a cast for a while. Her bone was splintered, but not seriously. It's very fortunate there was no harm done to your little one." She wrapped Kyoko's arm in a bandage to absorb some of the blood, then gave her a cup of water and a pain pill. "I'll need to step out for my supplies. This will help you with the pain."

As Dr. Wade left the room, Jasper approached Kyoko. "That looks pretty painful."

Kyoko winced. "It is. But the only thing that matters is the baby is safe."

Jasper held her, careful of her wounded arm. "I feel like Mom looked out for you tonight, trying to protect her grandchild." This whole incident reminded him of how much he missed his mother.

Kyoko nodded. "I feel the same way." She paused. "Why don't we name the baby Nancy, after your mother? I think it would be a fitting tribute, don't you?"

Jasper looked into her eyes, overwhelmed with emotion. "That means a lot to me, Ky. You and this baby are the most important people in my life."

"It's the least I can do for the woman who gave me you." She stroked his face gently.

Dr. Wade came in, followed by a nurse pushing a cart full of supplies. Jasper, Terri, and Annette watched as she performed the delicate task of putting Kyoko's arm in a cast.

"Alright," Dr. Wade announced, as she secured the cast. "You're all set, Mrs. Holdron." She jotted a prescription onto her pad and handed it to Kyoko. "Make sure you stop by the pharmacy and have this filled. Go easy on the housework, and no heavy lifting." She stood, shaking Jasper's hand. "I'm counting on you to make sure she follows my orders."

Jasper nodded. He would make it a top priority that his wife was well-rested. "That won't be a problem. Thanks, Doc."

"You're very welcome. I'll call for a follow up in about three weeks. I know you're due soon."

Jasper helped Kyoko to her feet, but she hesitated.

"We're not leaving, are we? We have to wait for Skye."

Even with her own injuries, she was very concerned about her sister-in law. Jasper loved that about her.

"We will. But let's get you something to eat." Jasper led Kyoko to the cafeteria, followed by Annette and Terri. After Kyoko had a light snack, the group filed into the ICU waiting room, taking seats near Lawrence, Delva and Cammie. After they had spoken briefly, the ding of the elevator caught everyone's attention. As the doors slid open, a disheveled Wayne stepped off. Spotting Cammie, he jogged over to her.

"Oh, baby," he whispered as he held her close. "Tara called me. I'm so glad you're okay. How are you, Kyoko?" he asked, sitting down next to Cammie.

"I'm fine. Actually, I think the painkillers are kicking in."

"What about Skye? Was she really shot twice? Who would do that to her?"

"Yes, and she should be coming out of surgery any minute now." Lawrence's expression clearly showed his anger as he spoke the next sentence. "And the bastard who did this to her better hope the police find him before I do." He balled his fists so tightly his knuckles turned white.

Wayne turned to Cammie. "What in the world happened?"

"We were coming out of the country club after my shower, and we were just standing in the parking lot, talking. The next thing I know, I heard Skye scream...there was so much blood... and then Kyoko..." Cammie's voice trailed off, and Wayne placed a comforting arm around her.

"I think I've heard enough," Wayne declared. "I'm ready to join with Jasper and Lawrence in serving this guy a triple portion of whoop-ass. Someone could have been killed!" He turned his urgent eyes on the love of his life. "I could have lost you."

Kyoko was the voice of reason. "Alright, guys. He's not my favorite person, either. But let the police handle him. I don't want to have to bail my husband and his friends out of the Iron Bar Inn."

Jasper made a suggestion. "Okay, we'll give the police a two day head start. If they haven't found him by then, we go looking for him and beat his sorry ass beyond recognition."

Lawrence and Wayne nodded, reluctantly agreeing not to pound on Pope's face until the police at least had a chance to arrest him.

Silence fell over the group. The quiet was broken by the sound of Dr. Lee, shuffling down the hall in his surgery scrubs and paper shoes.

"Mr. Holdron, you can see your wife now. She's in recovery. Are there any other relatives present?" He glanced around at the small crowd gathered in the nearby seats.

Delva stood. "I'm her sister."

She followed Dr. Lee and Lawrence into Skye's room. As Lawrence was about to approach the bed, Dr. Lee stopped him, pulling him aside.

He spoke softly. "She did very well during the surgery. With about three to five weeks of bed rest, she should heal very nicely. But there's something else I need to make you aware of. This may be very difficult for you to hear." The doctor sighed, and his discomfort was obvious.

Lawrence tensed visibly. "What do you mean? You just said she would be fine. What am I missing here?"

Silence ruled for a few moments.

"While I was performing the surgery," Dr. Lee began, his face somber, "I removed an embryo."

Chapter 16
November 2005

Lawrence was confused for a moment before coming to a horrible realization. "You mean, a baby? Skye was pregnant?"

Dr. Lee sighed. "Yes, she was in the early stages. I'd say she was about four weeks along. Unfortunately, with the injuries she sustained -- I'm sorry. The embryo could not be saved. But please know that you should have no trouble conceiving in the future."

Cammie gasped, clasping a hand over her mouth in horror and shock. Delva wiped at the tears streaming down her face.

Lawrence screamed, his rage and pain filling the room. "I'll kill him!" He dropped to his knees, sobbing. His entire body shook with the crushing reality of what he'd heard.

Dr. Lee approached Skye, who was now almost fully awake. He delivered the news to her as gently as she could. Moments later, her anguished cries could be heard from each end of the corridor.

"My baby..." she moaned. "How could he take my baby..."

Lawrence rose from the floor, his body heavy with sadness. He lay next to Skye in the hospital bed, cradling her. No one present knew what to say, so they left them alone. Skye and Lawrence were left to grieve for the child they would never meet.

*

It was a long drive home the next day. Skye and

Lawrence rode most of the way in silence. She dozed in the passenger seat, drowsy from the combination of painkillers and a heavy heart. Finally, Lawrence spoke.

"Baby," he began. "I should have killed him that day at Barham Park. I wish I had."

Skye surveyed the red rimmed, damp eyes of her husband. "You can't blame yourself for this, Lawrence." She sighed. "Just be here for me."

Pulling into their driveway, he cut the engine and gazed at Skye. "I just hate that things went down like this. I mean, we didn't even know you were pregnant."

Skye looked down at the dressings on her abdomen. "Dr. Lee said we can conceive in the future. We'll try again, when the time comes." She tried to sound hopeful, even though she felt as if a part of her soul had been ripped from her.

Lawrence got out and went around to the passenger side of the car. Unbuckling her seat belt, he lifted his wife from the seat and closed the car door with his foot. Once they were inside the house, he carried her upstairs to the bedroom, where he laid her down as gently as possible. She gazed up at him, her brown eyes like two melancholy pools.

"I'm too weak and sore to make love to you," she said. "Lay next to me."

With all the care and concern he felt, Lawrence undressed her. After helping her into a nightgown, he shed his clothing and joined her on the bed. There he kissed and caressed her until she was asleep in his arms.

Lawrence reached to the bedside table for the remote and turned on the television. Keeping the volume low so he wouldn't disturb Skye, he scanned the channels for a local news report. On Channel Five, he found what he was looking for.

"Breaking news out of Boca Raton today," the female

anchor announced. "As Palm Beach County authorities search for Maurice Gregory Pope, thirty-four, of Chicago. Pope is wanted in connection with last night's shooting at the Boca Raton Country Club. Two women, leaving a gathering at the club, were injured."

Footage rolled across the screen, showing the aftermath of the shooting. "I was walking out for a cigarette break, and I heard the shots," a middle-aged bartender for the country club said to an interviewer. "I just dropped to the ground."

The evening anchor reappeared on screen. "A sighting was reported of Pope in the area near Barham Park this evening, but he has since disappeared. Anyone with information should contact the police immediately. Pope is considered armed and dangerous."

Disgusted, Lawrence turned off the television and lay down next to Skye.

If they don't find him in the next few days, Jasper, Wayne and I will, he thought, as he drifted into a restless sleep. And we won't be hospitable.

*

The Monday following the shooting, Cammie opened the office at nine sharp, as Skye requested. The firm was backed up with jobs, and they couldn't afford to close the office down during the three weeks Skye would be out. So Cammie, along with Annette and James, vowed to keep the business running in her absence.

Cammie sat at the desk in the reception area, thumbing through the manila folder Skye gave her. It was filled with design sketches and detailed notes. Cammie had no design experience, except for the short time she covered for Terri, so the folder was her guide. Skye assured her she'd do fine, as long as she and the assistants worked together and followed her sketches.

Around nine thirty, James entered the office, with Annette close behind him. "Good morning, Ms. Hamlin," he said, as he took her place behind the desk. "I hope I'll be as good as you at handling the office."

"I'm sure you'll do well, James," Cammie assured him. "As long as you're courteous and helpful, things will be fine." She turned to Annette. "Well, it looks like it's just you, me, and the sketches."

"Cool, Ms. H," Annette chirped. "I'm ready to get started whenever you are."

"Good. Our first stop today is Oasis Spa. There are a few things that were left unfinished there, some window treatments and wall décor."

"Okay." Annette nodded. "Let's go."

On the way out, Cammie turned to James. "We'll be back around lunchtime."

"Okay, Ms. Hamlin," he called out.

Cammie and Annette left for the Oasis Spa, the first of many jobs they would handle while Skye recovered.

*

"Ugh, Skye grunted as she attempted to reach the remote control. It was mid November, and she was prone on the sofa, watching TV. She had one more week before she due back at work, and she was bored silly.

Hearing her, Lawrence rushed in from the kitchen. "Oh, no you don't, little Missy." He handed her the remote from the side table.

Skye rolled her eyes, but smiled inwardly. "Thanks, Warden."

"Hey," Lawrence countered. "I'm trying to take good

care of you. You need to rest up and heal if you want to go back to work next week."

"I know. I'm so bored." She sighed as she flipped through the channels. "There's nothing on." Exasperated, she turned the television off.

"Are you hungry? Thirsty?"

"I'm fine, Lawrence." Skye lovingly stroked his face. "You've been just wonderful these past few weeks."

"I feel like I need to make up to you for the way I've been acting." He looked down at the floor guiltily.

"It's okay, baby..."

"No," he said, sitting at her feet. "It's not. I should have let you know how I was feeling, instead of hiding in my office all the time. But I was under so much stress to perform at work, plus I had to be your hero."

Skye looked into his eyes. "You know I didn't mean to put so much pressure on you."

Lawrence nodded. "I know. But that doesn't matter anymore." He grasped her hand and placed it over his heart. "Now that all this has happened, I realize that I love protecting you. You are the best and brightest thing in my life. And after losing a baby, and almost losing you, I love you more than ever."

Skye didn't fight the tears rolling down her cheeks. "Oh, Lawrence. I love you, too. We're going to figure this out somehow. I know it."

"Well, I've already started," Lawrence said, his eyes and tone turning serious. "I've been asking you to see a therapist for years now, and you haven't. So I found one for you. Her name is Dr. Rose Blanchard, and I've scheduled an appointment for you on the twenty-second." He watched her face for a reaction. "It's not negotiable anymore. I love you too much to keep watching you suffer."

Skye accepted his reasoning. "Fine. I'll go." She shook

her head. "I know it's time, and I'm sorry I've been so stubborn."

Lawrence took his wife gently into his arms. "Thank you, baby."

Skye laughed, wiping away her tears. "I should be thanking you." She winced as the laughter caused a dull pain in her abdomen.

"Are you in pain?" He watched her intently.

"Just a little bit. I forgot I shouldn't laugh so hard."

"Let me see if I can help..."

His voice trailed off as he pressed his lips to hers. She opened her mouth and he fed on her sweetness for a few torrid moments before pulling away. Lowering himself, he lifted her tee shirt and pressed his lips against the tender flesh around her bandaged scar.

"Lawrence," she whispered breathlessly, "you know I can't make love yet..."

"I know," he murmured into her soft skin. "But you can let me please you..."

Trailing his kisses lower, he used his large hands to undo the drawstring on her gray sweatpants. Skye gingerly lifted her hips, allowing him to remove the pants, along with the cotton boy shorts underneath. When she was naked from the waist down, he trailed his long fingers along her bare thighs. She shivered beneath his touch.

"When you look at your scar, you'll remember only this," he whispered, his breath warm as he nuzzled her belly button.

His words disappeared into her flesh as he kissed the dark patch of curls at the apex of her thighs. He drifted lower, slowly and skillfully licking the tight bud sheltered there. Above him, Skye cooed with pleasure, her thighs parting in unabashed invitation.

Smiling, he whispered, "You have no idea how much I love you..." He accented his statement with one spine-tingling lick. "Let me show you..."

He brought both hands to her thighs, opening her as widely as he could. Her nectar flowed, the entrance to his private paradise glistening . He dipped his tongue into the passage, savoring the taste of her arousal, then continued his loving assault on her. Even though his manhood throbbed with need, he ignored it. This was about her; he would heal her with his own special brand of medicine.

Skye's world was spinning. She was slipping off the couch, but she didn't care. He caught her, keeping her from falling. Each pass of his tongue, each suckle of his lips pushed her closer and closer to release. Finally, she could stand it no longer and she came, screaming and writhing and shaking .

She came back to herself and looked down into Lawrence's passion-hooded eyes. She beckoned to him with a finger and he rose to meet her. There on the sofa, with the faint light of the setting sun shining on them, she kissed him with all the love and appreciation she felt.

*

November 22nd, three weeks and two days after the shooting, Skye finally went back to the office. She hummed to herself as she dressed in a yellow shell and mint colored pants suit. She wore flats, on Dr. Lee's orders, until she was strong enough to walk in heels again. Her hair was pinned back, except for a few loose curls around her face. That morning, she lovingly kissed Lawrence's scruffy, unshaven face. As she left the house, Skye was excited at the prospect of doing what she loved once again. When she arrived, Cammie was once again sitting at the reception desk to greet her.

"Hey, girl," Cammie said, rising from her chair to hug Skye. "How are you feeling?"

"I'm fine, and you should know that. You've been at my house almost every day for the past few weeks. Thanks for being such a big help."

"No problem, Skye. That's what friends do, right?" Cammie smiled, returning to her seat behind the desk. "Oh, you should probably go look in your office. Some things came for you while you were out." A sly smile graced her lips, and Skye started to wonder what was stashed in there.

Skye walked slowly down the corridor and unlocked her office. Inside, she found a room full of balloons, cards and floral arrangements. She was touched at the outpouring of well wishes from family, friends, neighbors, and colleagues alike. Even Senator York had sent her a lovely arrangement of sterling roses.

Approaching the largest bouquet of the bunch, she admired its beauty. It was an array of bear grass, calla lilies, and white and yellow roses, her favorites. Opening the attached card, she read the message inside.

'To the best big sister in the world. You have taught me so much about unconditional love. Delva.'

Pleasantly surprised, Skye sat down at her desk and made a phone call to thank Delva.

"Hey, Delva," Skye said, when she answered the phone. "The flowers are absolutely beautiful. I really appreciate them." And she did. It was refreshing to see Delva going out of her way to be kind to her. "So, how's life back home with Mom and Dad?"

"It's great. I've missed them a lot. And trust me, Skye," Delva countered sincerely, "the flowers were the very least I could do. I just hope we can have a good relationship from now on."

"Well, you're already forgiven, that's a start. I'm

willing to work on being friends with you. So, where are Mom and Dad?"

"Mama's teaching a world literature class, and Daddy said he was going downstairs to his office to do some paperwork. You know, I've been thinking about working with him, as his receptionist. That way, he could spend more time doing what he loves, while I handle the administrative stuff."

"I think that's a great idea," Skye admitted, as she went through the stack of mail in her in-box "I think it would be a good arrangement for both of you."

"I want to help out. I'm grateful Mom and Dad didn't disown me. I'm going to ask him about it later." Delva was running water. "I was just starting to wash dishes, so I'll call you later, okay?"

"Sure. Bye, Delva."

As Skye place the receiver into the cradle, she noticed Annette standing in her office doorway, patiently waiting.

"Yes, Annette."

"Mrs. Holdron, we have a new contract. They'd actually like us to start the job today."

"Who is this job for?"

"It's a master bedroom remodel for a Maxwell Levy. He says you know each other."

"Yes, he's a partner at the law firm my husband works for." She paused. "Give me a few minutes to look over the paperwork he filled out, and we'll leave when I'm finished." She accepted the papers Annette placed on her desk. "By the way, thank you for the flowers."

"You're welcome, Mrs. H." The young woman smiled as she exited the office.

About an hour later, Skye, along with Annette and her other assistant, James, were arriving at Maxwell Levy's palatial estate in Hampton Hills. The long, cobblestone driveway led to the grandiose, stucco and stone Spanish style home. They were let into the house by the maid, who introduced herself as Lisa.

As Lisa escorted them up the spiral staircase to the master suite, Skye admired the many architectural details of the house -- the trey ceilings, the cream-colored crown molding throughout, and the hand laid, imported tile. She delighted in the feel of the highly polished walnut handrail as they made their ascent. Wow. This is going to be a challenging job, she thought, relishing the chance to work on a house with such a unique design.

The master suite did not disappoint. It was just as well appointed as the rest of the house. But Maxwell's wife had expressed an interest in changing the color scheme in the room, as well as updating the bathroom with more romantic elements.

Skye addressed Lisa. "Thank you for showing us in." She turned to her assistants. "Let's get started."

*

Later that evening, Skye was lying on a chaise in the office of Dr. Rose Blanchard. After her talk with Lawrence, Skye decided it was time she sought therapy to help her deal with the traumatic events she endured.

"Okay, Mrs. Holdron. I know about the shooting, and other events of the past several months," Dr. Blanchard stated, turning the page on her notepad, "why don't you tell me where all the drama with Mr. Pope first started? This will give me some insight into what triggers your panic attacks, which will help me treat them effectively." She sat back, her posture casual and unassuming, to encourage Skye to vent her thoughts.

"I can't, Dr. Blanchard," Skye said, feeling the familiar burning in her chest. "I've never been able to talk about it.

Please, don't make me..." Her body shivered as she began to weep, unable to stifle the overwhelming emotion.

Dr. Blanchard placed a comforting hand on her shoulder. "It's perfectly all right you feel that way. Would you give your consent for me to hypnotize you? It may be the least painful way for me to learn more about the circumstances."

Skye nodded wearily. If she could finally purge her soul, without being mentally present, then hypnosis would be ideal.

"Good. Now, Mrs. Holdron, I need you to lie back on the chaise and close your eyes. Listen very carefully to the sound of my voice."

Skye did as she was asked, muttering, "Call me Skye, Doctor."

"Very well. Skye, I want you to slowly begin to sink into a deep state of relaxation. First, relax your arms and legs. Then, let the tension escape from your shoulders, your neck, your back, and your hips. Release all tension from your body as you sink deeper and deeper into pleasant relaxation." Dr. Blanchard readied her notepad. "You feel very light now, like you are floating on air. You are calm, and filled with feelings of warmth and comfort."

Skye was entranced; her arms and legs hanging limply off the chaise.

Chapter 17
September 1989

"It's packed as hell up in here," Skye commented to her roommate, Valencia Parker. They entered the annual Omega Psi Phi Roll-out Party at NCCU in Durham, North Carolina. She estimated at least five hundred rowdy college students packed into the student union, shaking their asses to "Give It to Me, Baby," sung by the illustrious Rick James.

"I know that's right," Valencia responded, shouting over the loud music. Tugging on the hem of her belted tank top, she scanned the crowd for her boyfriend. "There's Dante. I promised I would meet him here. Do you mind?"

"No," Skye yelled. "I'm gonna get something to drink, then cruise the scene. I'm cool."

Valencia waved and disappeared into the thick crowd. Skye slowly made her way to the bar, dodging the flailing hands and extended feet of random people. Taking a seat on the last vacant stool, she summoned the bartender. "Ginger ale on the rocks, please."

The bartender smiled. "Isn't it a little early for the hard stuff?" He chuckled as he went about fixing her drink.

Skye sensed someone watching her. Turning around, she saw the familiar faces of two of her classmates from Duke, Maurice Pope and the fine-as-hell Lawrence Holdron.

"Hey, Lawrence," Skye said, admiring his fly outfit and neatly trimmed box haircut. She couldn't hide the come-hither look on her face whenever she saw him. "Hello, Maurice," she continued, acknowledging Lawrence's constant companion briefly, then turning back to him. "How's senior year shaping up [for you]?"

Though Skye addressed Lawrence, Maurice answered. "Fine, so far. That is, as long as we come over here to get some exposure to our brothers and sisters from time to time. You know Duke is eighty percent white." He snorted, laughing at his own humor. When he realized no one would join him, he cut the chuckling short.

"Yeah," Skye said, still staring at Lawrence with obvious interest. They'd only had two classes together; Lawrence was pre-law and Skye was an accounting major. But she'd spent the better part of the last two years lusting after him. "What about you, Lawrence?"

He smiled, and Skye melted. "It's okay. I kind of miss Morehouse, but hey, it's almost over, right?" He leaned in close to Skye, and she could smell the intoxicating masculine scent of his cologne. "Plus, I got to meet a fine honey like you, so it wasn't all bad."

Maurice interjected. "Come on, Law. You sweet talkin' her when you know I was about to ask her to dance?" He put his hand over his heart, feigning injury. "You hurt my feelings, man."

Lawrence laughed. "What a coincidence. I was about to ask the same thing." He extended his hand to Skye. "Ms. Donovan, would you like to dance?"

"Sure," she replied, blushing as she took his hand. Lawrence led her to the dance floor as "Two Occasions," by The Deele, began to play. As they swayed, she ignored Maurice's dejected look.

The DJ spun more of the hits for the next few hours. After they finished shaking it to DJ Jazzy Jeff and the Fresh Prince's hit "Parents Just Don't Understand," Lawrence led Skye by the hand to an outdoor picnic table near the west side of the building.

They sat next to each other on the wooden bench. Skye gazed at the starry night.

"What's on your mind?" Lawrence's voice cut her daydreaming short. She turned her eyes toward his face, illuminated by the streetlight near the table.

"I've wanted to talk to you for months," Skye said quietly, "but Maurice is always with you. It's so obvious he has a crush on me, and I don't want to hurt his feelings."

"Wow." Lawrence grinned, shaking his head. "If I'd known that, I would have kicked him to the curb a long time ago. He only hangs around me because he wanted to go to Morehouse, but his parents weren't having it." He paused, chuckling. "I don't really care for him, but he thinks of me as his link to 'the Morehouse experience'."

Skye laughed, realizing for the first time how comfortable she felt with him. "Why would his parents forbid him from Morehouse?"

"They're uppity," Lawrence said in a matter of fact tone. "They wanted him at a white school. You know how rich folks can be." He stuck his nose in the air to emphasize his point. "I think it's sweet you tried to spare the poor sap's ego."

Skye giggled.

He touched her cheek, then turned her face up to his and kissed her softly.

She didn't push him away; she didn't want him to stop. Her lips parted, and she fed on his passion as his tongue probed her mouth. When he released her, she was panting and dazzled.

"I have to go," Skye whispered, standing. She pulled as notepad from her purse, jotted her number, then tore the sheet off. "Give me a call," she said, tossing the piece of paper at him and retreating, lest she be overtaken by desire.

Skye noted it was seven minutes after one , and sought out Valencia. Approaching the glass door on the east side of the building, she spotted Valencia in the crowd, and was just about to enter when Maurice stepped from the shadows. Startled, Skye jumped and backed away from him. Frantically looking around, she saw no one nearby.

"Well, well, Ms. Donovan," Maurice sneered, his face twisted in a frightening scowl. "I see you and my boy hit it off tonight." He closed the distance between them quickly, backing Skye up against the outer wall of the building.

"Maurice, what are you..." Skye began weakly, her voice trembling with fear.

"Shut up, skank," he hissed, his breath hot and foul from one drink too many. "I've been trying to talk to you ever since we were freshmen. I guess I'm not good enough for you, huh?"

Skye tried to scurry away , but Maurice grabbed her wrist, forcing her hand to the bulging crotch of his pants. When she recoiled, he slapped her with his free hand.

"Don't walk away from me when I'm talking to you, you uppity whore." He ignored the tears streaming down Skye's face as he pushed her toward the bushes near the back of the building. "I came out here tonight to offer you a gift, and you're gonna take it, whether you like it or not!"

Skye dared not struggle since he was twice her size and would just strike her again. She closed her eyes and prayed he wouldn't kill her when he was done with her. She heard a loud thwack, then a thud. Opening her eyes, she saw Maurice lying in a heap in front of her. A white girl she sort of recognized from school stood over him. Breathing hard, she gripped a smooth, wooden baseball bat in her hand. A splatter of Maurice's blood decorated the business end of it.

"Hey, are you all right?" The girl extended her hand to

Skye and pulled her out of the bushes.

"Yeah," Skye winced as she gingerly touched her bruised cheek. "Thank you. Haven't I seen you around Duke?"

"I'm Cammie Hamlin. I'm in your Principles of Marketing class." She glanced down at Maurice's limp body and gestured toward the parking lot. "I was on my way to my car when I saw the two of you. It looked a little suspect, so I got my bat and came closer. When I heard him threatening you, I swung away."

Skye looked at this girl, whom she'd barely spoken to at school and became overwhelmed with gratitude. "I don't know how to thank you. There's no telling what he would have done to me."

"Hey," Cammie patted her on the shoulder, "no problem. I hope someone would do it for me. This was the highlight of my week." She smiled, and Skye knew she made a lifelong friend.

Cammie walked Skye inside to find a security guard. In the space of fifteen minutes, the University Police and Durham Five-O were on the scene. Having taken Cammie and Skye's statements, they escorted a drunken, bruised, and semi-conscious Maurice away in handcuffs. A crowd gathered outside the student union to gawk at the scene. After they watched Maurice being carted away, Cammie and Skye exchanged numbers, and Valencia took Skye back to the apartment they shared off campus to ice her reddened cheek.

November 2005

"Now, Mrs. Holdron. When I snap my fingers, you will awake from your trance. You will feel totally relaxed and relieved of the burden of what you've just told me. One, two, three..."

Dr. Blanchard snapped her fingers, and Skye awoke. "Are you all right? Do you know where you are?"

"Yes, Dr. Blanchard," Skye said quietly as she sat up.

"And how do you feel?"

"I feel light, unburdened. Thank you, Doctor."

"I'm glad I could help you." She finished her notes. Then, she grabbed a pad from a locked drawer of the desk.

"I'll write a prescription for a mild sleep aid. I'm sure you'll need something to help you relax until Mr. Pope is in custody." She scribbled on the pad, ripping the sheet off and handing it to Skye. "But I think you will notice a marked improvement in your level of anxiety. Releasing the pressure of a traumatic event by talking about it can often have that effect."

Skye took the prescription, placing it in her purse. "Thank you again, Dr. Blanchard." She stood to leave.

"If you need to talk give me a call, and we'll set something up."

"I'd like to set up an appointment now. This has really helped me."

Dr. Blanchard gave Skye her appointment book, letting her fill in the time. Glancing at it when she was done, the doctor said, "Then I'll see you in a few days."

Skye left the doctor's office, feeling more empowered than she'd felt in fifteen years.

*

As evening fell, Pope was leaving a homeless shelter in Palm Beach. *Turns out this was a pretty good hiding place.* He hummed as he walked from the shelter to the bus station. He wore the few items of clothing they'd given him: a black jacket, black baseball cap, and worn blue jeans. A navy blue backpack was slung over his shoulder.

Pope stepped onto a transit bus, paid his fare, and took a seat near the rear. He sat back and relaxed, prepared for the ride to Boca Raton.

The darkness shrouding the Royal Oak Hills neighborhood later that night made it easy for Maurice to hide in the shadows. As he crept along, crouched low behind Skye and Lawrence's property, he remained soundless. Swinging his body over the seven-foot privacy fence, he dropped into the vegetable garden with a thud.

Finally able to stand, knowing the neighbors wouldn't be able to see him, Pope made his way along the perimeter, his back pressed against the white-washed wood. Pope was well aware he had to be extra careful, as getting in and out of Skye's house in total silence was his goal.

He stood outside the patio door, watching Skye get herself a bowl of ice cream from the freezer. He smiled. She was home alone.

No one's here to rescue you now. He picked the lock with the tools he'd been carrying in his pants pocket. *Time for you to pay for my humiliation, uppity whore.*

Pope knew the reason he was so desperate for revenge on Skye. His upbringing as the only child of a very wealthy family had been less than ideal. Pope knew his parents thought of him more as a liability than a son.

He attended the finest schools, owned the most expensive cars, had his pick of gold-digging women throughout high school and college. But deep inside, emptiness ruled. All his life, he was given everything.

Except real affection.

Then he met Skye.

There was just something about her, a glow of kindness and inner beauty that radiated from her. When he first saw her, he knew she was the key. Skye could love him in a way his mother never had. From that moment, he was consumed by the desire to be with her.

When she rejected him, cast him aside as his own mother had, Pope snapped. Nothing else mattered. He gritted his teeth, determined to make Skye pay for refusing his advances.

His thoughts drifted for a moment, back to the day he discovered just how little his parents cared about him. He often heard his parents speak ill of him when they thought he wasn't around. They would go back and forth about what a disappointment he was, and how much he "complicated" things for them. By the time he left for college, Pope was so numb he no longer cared.

But that didn't stop him from being utterly amazed at his parent's actions on the day he was released from jail back in 'Ninety-Three.

Chapter 18
October 1993

It was seven o'clock on a bright and brisk morning, and Deloris Anne Bennet-Pope rushed into the North Carolina Men's Correctional Facility in Raleigh. Her dyed jet-black hair was covered with a printed silk scarf, her face obscured by large, dark sunglasses as she entered the lobby. Though she was out of the glaring sunlight, she didn't remove her shades as she approached the reception desk.

"Good morning, sir," she said, greeting the uniformed officer behind the desk with her usual mix of fake cheerfulness and charm school propriety. "I'm here to for my son, Maurice Pope. He's being released today." She hoped to convey her desire for privacy through her hushed tone.

"Okay, ma'am." The officer smiled knowingly, seeming to sense her embarrassment. "I'll need to see some I.D., and you'll need to sign the log book. Then we can turn your son, and his belongings, over to you."

Quickly, Delores handed the officer her Illinois driver's license, then produced a gold plated pen from her crocodile handbag and scribbled her signature in the log book. She followed the officer to a holding cell, where Pope sat, elbows resting on a wooden table. The large orange envelope containing his belongings lay on the table in front of him.

When Pope saw his mother enter, he approached her eagerly. "Mother!"

Delores deflected his oncoming embrace with her hand. "Do be careful of my makeup, dear." She gave him an air kiss on each cheek and patted his shoulder. "If you're ready, I'd like to leave this dreadful place as quickly as possible."

Pope sighed. His mother was just as vain and emotionally dead as ever. "Yes, Mother. I'm ready." Retrieving his envelope from the table, he followed his mother to the black sedan outside.

Nodding to the driver, Pope slid into the backseat next to Delores. During the ride to RDU International Airport, he spoke little. There was no need. With Delores' constant complaining about how much of a disgrace he was to the family, he couldn't get a word in. So he threw in a few obligatory "You're right, Mother" statements, but otherwise rode in reflective silence.

Delores' verbal assault would have continued on their flight to Chicago, but upon entering the family's private plane, Delores announced she was "terribly tired and upset," and retired to the sleeping chamber in the back of the aircraft.

Reveling in the silence after his mother sequestered herself, Pope reclined in his seat, sipping a glass of champagne. I'm gonna need something harder than this, he mused, as he pictured his father's angry face. Nathan Amadeus Pope was displeased when he discovered his only son would serve four years in prison for attempted rape and assault. Pope was aware his father's anger was less about the crimes he committed, and more about the potential embarrassment the family would face.

Pope knew his father would be waiting at the door of the family's palatial estate, ready with the lecture to end all lectures. He was in no mood to hear Nathan's barking, but it couldn't be helped.

So Maurice helped himself to another glass of champagne, and two shots of Jack Daniels, before the plane touched down in Chicago.

Sure enough, Nathan waited in the foyer when Delores and a reluctant Maurice entered. Delores immediately went to her bedroom, leaving Maurice alone with his visibly upset father.

Dropping onto the nearest Victorian settee, Pope laid back and prepared for the onslaught.

Pacing the marble floor, Nathan Pope was truly an imposing figure. His wide, six foot three, smartly dressed frame seemed to block the incoming sunlight. As he paced, he rubbed his salt and pepper beard, choosing his words carefully.

"Maurice, I'm sure your mother already expressed our mutual disdain for your behavior. I hope you're aware of the trouble you've caused."

"Yes, sir," he mumbled, staring at his feet.

"Straighten up, and look at me when I'm speaking to you, son," Nathan rumbled. Pope quickly assumed proper posture. "Now," Nathan continued, "we've made some decisions while you were...away. In order to keep your inheritance, you'll be required to finish your schooling. We'll expect you to obtain your medical degree in Dermatology, just as you planned to do before you had that colossal lapse in judgment."

"Yes, sir. I thought I'd transfer to Morehouse, and..."

"That's out of the question. You know your mother and I don't want you attending some low-rate black college in the south."

Maurice persisted. "But, Dad, I..."

"Don't continue to test me, boy. I'll accompany you down to the University next week to get you enrolled. When you've finished your degree, we'll purchase some property for you. You'll go into private practice there. My lawyer has assured me that no one will question us about your record if we do things this way. Everything I've just told you has already been set in motion, it's nonnegotiable. Do you understand, Maurice?"

"Yes, sir," Pope answered, wilting under his father's disapproving glare. "Why are you doing this?"

"It's not for you, I can assure you." Nathan sat down next to his young son. "We've got to get your life back on track to avoid any further embarrassment. There's no reason your mistakes should ruin me and LornaCorp. Reputation is very important in the pharmaceuticals industry. My poor mother must be spinning in her grave with your foolishness on the verge of tarnishing her legacy."

Pope watched, his mouth hanging open, as Nathan stood and stalked away. His parents orchestrated his entire life, down to the last detail, just to keep up appearances. As he turned it over in his mind, Maurice couldn't help laughing.

Soon his hysterical laughter filled the east wing of the Pope estate.

November 2005

Snapping himself to the present, Pope focused on the task at hand. A few calculated moves later, he pressed against the wall in the darkened kitchen. Skye was upstairs with her ice cream. Striding across the linoleum floor to the base of the stairway, he listened for any sign of Lawrence's pickup truck approaching. Hearing nothing but the television in the master bedroom, he crept silently up the stairs.

Crouching low outside the bedroom door, he could see Skye, propped up on a pile of pillows, watching TV. Her empty ice cream bowl was on the nightstand next to her. Pope let his eyes travel the outline of her womanly body in the thin, lavender silk nightgown she wore. She was so beautiful he almost salivated.

Skye suddenly jumped, as if she felt his eyes on her. "Lawrence, is that you?" She waited for a reply. Hearing nothing, she stuck her hand underneath the pile of pillows she reclined on, and went back to a rerun of "Charlie's Angels."

Seizing the opportunity when she let her guard down, Pope burst into the room. "Hello, Skye. How's my favorite uppity whore?"

Skye growled. "What the hell are you doing here, Pope? Shouldn't you be in jail, being the girlfriend of some convict named Big John?"

Pope scoffed. "Oh, you got jokes. But that smart mouth is gonna get you in trouble." He approached her slowly. "Lawrence isn't here to protect you, and neither is that white girl." Reaching out, he stroked her nearly bare breast. "So what have you got to back up that mouth of yours, huh?"

Skye smiled. "I was hoping you'd provoke me." Her left hand swung out to grab his right arm, then she pulled a shiny Louisville Slugger from beneath the pile of pillows. "This is what I've to back it up."

She swung the bat with all the force she could muster, and it made a sickening crack as it connected with Pope's skull. He recoiled, staggering as he clutched his bleeding forehead. He cursed when he noticed she was out of bed.

"You bitch!" He lunged, but was too dizzy to make contact with her. He couldn't get his bearings in the now revolving room.

Skye had been to six more sessions with Dr. Blanchard, and the therapist's words echoed in her mind: You have the right and the ability to protect yourself.

She turned an angry gaze on Pope. "Oh, I got your bitch right here." She swung again, this time taking out his right knee, sending him crashing to the floor. "When I heard you were evading the police, I figured your crazy ass would try to pull something like this." Skye realized she was in control of the situation, and she relished it. She swung the bat again, connecting with the tender flesh of his abdomen. His scream of agony rose over the sound of the television. "What did you think, Pope? I was gonna let you rape me? Brutalize me in my own house? Oh, hell no!" She accentuated her point on the last phrase by shoving the end of the bat into his testicles.

"OWWWWWWW! GOD!" Pope howled in pain as Skye turned the family jewels into glistening dust. "Damn you, whore!"

"No, Pope. Damn you." She raised the bat one more time, and smacked him in the back of the head, knocking him unconscious.

Sweaty and breathing heavily, Skye picked up the

cordless phone next to the bed to call the police. While she waited for them, she did a few victory laps around her bedroom, never once taking her eyes off the prone Pope. If he moved, she was ready to pop him again.

*

When Lawrence came home, he was shocked to find his front yard and house full of the men in blue. The sight of the ambulance parked at the curb made his insides twist. Skye, he thought, terrified. Pushing past them to get into the house, he burst into the bedroom, just in time to see the paramedics loading Pope onto a stretcher. He was a pitiful sight, moaning in agony, blood running down his pain-contorted face.

Skye sat on the bed, breathing hard, but smiling. In her hand was a Louisville Slugger.

Curious, he turned to his wife. "Baby, did you do that? He looks like he lost a fight with some farm machinery."

Skye held up the bloody bat, mopping the sweat from her forehead. "Yep. I borrowed this from Cammie."

"Now that's my girl."

Lawrence hugged his wife tightly. "I'm proud of you. You opened a giant can of whoop-ass on him."

"I did, didn't I?" Skye's face filled with relief.

Lawrence shook his head in amazement. It looked like she conquered her anxiety.

The rest of the night was filled with activity. Lawrence watched as Skye calmly answered all the questions the police asked her. Once the officer was satisfied with her description of the events, he took the baseball bat she was still clutching.

"Gotta take this downtown for processing," the officer explained, placing the Slugger in a large plastic bag with his gloved hand.

"No problem. Just let me know when I can get it back. It belongs to a good friend." Skye waved as the officer departed.

*

Pope was hospitalized for two weeks as his broken body struggled to heal from the beat down he received. On the night they'd admitted him, he was out cold. But the next morning, he summoned his nurse. "Could you call my mother and tell her where I am?"

The nurse obliged, and Pope recited the number from his cell phone as she dialed it. "Mrs. Delores Pope? Yes, this is Myra King. I'm a nurse at Boca Raton Community Hospital in Florida. I just wanted to notify you that your son is in our care..."

"What's happened to him now?" Delores groused.

"We'll ma'am, the police told us he was attacked by a woman whose house he broke into. He's seriously injured..."

"I've got an appointment at the spa tomorrow; I don't have time to come all the way down there to see that boy," Delores interrupted again. "Besides, if he's going to behave like a common criminal, he should accept the consequences. Serves him right, the little miscreant." She disconnected the call.

He did have one visitor, though. As soon as he was well enough to walk again, a Palm Beach County Sheriff's deputy waited for him, ready to escort him to jail.

Chapter 19
December 2005

Downtown, in the offices of Levy, Howe, and Rupert, Lawrence was in the conference room, reading over paperwork involving the case the state of Florida was bringing against Maurice Pope. Sitting across from him at the large table was his friend, boss, and founding member of the firm, Alan Rupert.

Where did he get that suit? Lawrence wondered silently, surveying the well cut black suit he wore.

Alan leaned back in his leather executive chair, removing his reading glasses and rubbing his deep brown eyes. "I think this case is going to be a slam dunk for the state. And with Harold and I representing your wife and sister-in-law in the civil suit, you know we're going to convince the judge to shake this guy down for every asset he's got." He scratched his goatee thoughtfully.

Lawrence shook his head. "I don't know. I agree with you about the civil case; I'm not worried about that. But I have a feeling he's going to plead guilty, so he can get off with a lesser sentence."

Alan nodded. "Cheniqua Gray from Gray and Hill is representing him, and I have no doubt she'll advise him to take the guilty plea. It would be judicial suicide to do otherwise." He thumbed through the stack of papers in front of him. "But look at the charges. Two counts of assault with a deadly weapon, with intent to kill, two counts of aggravated assault, involuntary manslaughter for the unborn child of Mrs. Holdron, assault on a police officer, resisting arrest... The list is mighty long. And since he has a prior record of violence and attempted rape, there's no way any judge would give him less than thirty years. Aside from that, his chances of getting parole are slim to none."

Their conversation was interrupted by Alan's ringing cell phone. "Excuse me," he addressed Lawrence, and then answered the call. "Hello?"

Lawrence waited for Alan to finish his short conversation. When he closed his cell phone, Alan turned to Lawrence.

"That was Harold. Apparently, Cheniqua Gray is just as intelligent as we thought. Pope entered a guilty plea. He'll be arraigned within the week."

Lawrence sighed as a mixture of relief and anticipation came over him. "I can't wait to see that bastard fry in court. This time, his parents won't be able to clean up his mess for him."

"We've got six days to the arraignment, then another three weeks until we bring the civil case before..." he opened his briefcase, and removed a sheet of paper, reading the name from it. "...Judge Reginald Pettiford. "

*

Five days later, Maurice Pope sat in a briefing room at the Main Detention Center in West Palm Beach, waiting for his lawyer to arrive. His visible bruises still persisted, and he'd suffered loss of hearing in his left ear, but he'd been very lucky to come out of that hospital with testicles intact after what Skye did to him. Pope couldn't really blame her for what she'd done; the blows to the head seemed to have given him some new-found mental clarity on the situation. He'd also been informed by the doctor that he wouldn't be able to father any children, but that was a moot point, since he'd likely be in prison for the rest of his life.

The lawyer his father secured for him entered the room after fifteen minutes passed. Cheniqua Gray was a dark skinned island girl from the Bahamas, with a tall, curvy frame and sincere brown eyes. Her dark hair was pulled up and away from her face, and she looked professional in her navy blue pantsuit and gray camisole top. When she sat down across from him, her expression told Pope she was the bearer of bad news.

"What?" Pope asked. "What's going to happen next?"

"Maurice," she began, cautiously, "you have already revealed to me that you were the shooter on the night in question. And after your forcible entry into Mrs. Holdron's house, you've pretty much sealed your fate. There was no other option for you besides a guilty plea. That's the only chance you had to reduce your sentence."

Pope nodded, accepting her advice. "I know you're right. I've accepted that I'm going to prison. The only question is, for how long."

"I can't really say. But I do know the DA won't hesitate to bring up your past criminal history, and that's not going to help matters for you." She cleared her throat. "And there's more. Skye Holdron was apparently pregnant at the time of the shooting, and she miscarried. The DA has added involuntary manslaughter to the list of charges."

Pope's eyes widened as the realization of what he'd done came crashing down on him. "She was pregnant?" He had no idea. My God, I've taken an innocent life. The Asian woman's belly was visible, so he'd tried to avoid hitting her. But he never considered Skye could be carrying.

Cheniqua sighed. "Yes. This is very serious, Maurice. The shortest amount of time you can hope to serve is twenty-five years, and getting that sentence would be a long shot. Also," she shuffled through some papers she had brought. "Both Skye Holdron and Kyoko Yamanaka-Holdron are bringing civil suits against you. They are asking for over a half million dollars each in damages, medical bills, and for pain and suffering."

Pope couldn't look into the face of the woman defending him. Shame kept him from lifting his head. "I'll have to liquidate my assets....sell my practice. Just give them whatever they want. Don't fight them." As Cheniqua was about to protest, he stopped her. "We both know they deserve everything I have, and more. Nothing can make up for what I did to them. Especially Skye..."

He trailed off, not knowing what else to say. Cheniqua nodded her understanding of his wishes. "Your criminal case will be tried by Judge Theodora Carter, and she's tough. Write up a statement for her, and I'll pick it up before court, okay?"

That said, Cheniqua exited the room quietly.

The guards soon escorted Pope back to his cell, where he had the rest of the day to think about the life he'd taken. For the first time since 1989, Maurice Gregory Pope wrestled guilt. Everything he'd done to Skye weighed on him more heavily than anything he ever felt. He lay on the hard bed, staring at the gray concrete ceiling, until the sun went down, and rose again.

The next day, local camera crews and reporters descended upon the U.S. District Courthouse of Southern Florida in Miami like flies on a landfill. Pope couldn't ignore it as he was escorted, in shackles, through the throng of eager journalists to the courtroom where his arraignment would take place. Upon entering the room, he was greeted by the unsympathetic faces of those in attendance, including the Donovans and people who saw the shooting take place. But no face in the crowd was as angry and unpleasant as that of Lawrence Holdron. All these people showed up here, just to see my ass roasted on a spit. Pope dropped heavily into his seat next to his lawyer.

The bailiff approached the center of the room and announced loudly, "All Rise. The Honorable Theodora Carter, presiding."

A petite, light skinned woman in judicial robes breezed into the judge's box from the chambers. As soon as she was seated, her serious eyes landed on District Attorney Mendoza Alston.

"Counsel Alston, the charges against Mr. Pope are many, and very serious. I assume the state is prepared to meet the burden of proof?" Her tone was much more imposing than her small frame.

Inherently confident in his case, Mendoza didn't hesitate. "We are, Your Honor. We collected a great deal of evidence, including Mr. Pope's past history of violence, statements from both witnesses and victims of said violence, and several pieces of indisputable physical evidence." He straightened his patterned Gucci tie, indicating he'd made his point.

Judge Carter nodded. "Very well." She turned to Cheniqua. "Counsel Gray, I understand your client wishes to enter a guilty plea?"

"Yes, your honor. We have discussed this plea with District Attorney Alston."

"We agreed to a reduction of five to ten years from Mr. Pope's sentence, in exchange for his plea," Mendoza countered, presenting some papers from his brown leather attaché case.

"I see no need to waste taxpayer money by dragging these proceedings out, Mr. Pope," Judge Carter said, addressing Maurice. "You were wise to follow Counsel Gray's advice. I'll take some time to review the evidence the state has collected. Then I'll deliver my decision on the sentence. This court is in recess until nine tomorrow morning." She banged her gavel, and reentered her chambers.

As Pope was escorted from the courtroom, Delva approached him. "I can't believe how evil you are," she began, "and I can't believe you almost dragged me down with you. You should be ashamed of yourself."

Pope nodded. He didn't dispute her; he acted out of hatred, and was ashamed of his actions. The officer lead him away, back to the jail house where his only company were guilt and regret.

*

From a distance, Alan Rupert watched Delva as she spoke with Pope. He was captivated by her beauty; she was full of vivacity and determination. I know she's been through some things, and she's made some foolish choices, but I think all she really needs is a man to love her the right way. Alan decided that if he could tame this wild rose, he would be that man.

As the crowd dispersed, Alan approached Delva. "Miss Donovan, a moment of your time?'

Turning to face him, Delva smiled. "Sure, Mr. Rupert."

"Whoa, now," Alan said, with mock embarrassment. "Mr. Rupert is my father. Just call me Alan." He paused, drinking in her features. "Would you like to join me for a cup of coffee?"

"I'd love to." Delva linked arms with Alan, and he escorted her out of the courthouse.

*

The Java Joint was a hip spot about two blocks away. Although she knew of it, Delva had never been there. But as she and Alan entered the place and found a secluded table near the back of the establishment, she immediately like its vibe. The Moroccan theme, gold leaf paint job and rich shades of burgundy and orange, made for a very relaxed atmosphere.

She eased herself onto the orange cushion of the booth, and Alan dropped his briefcase onto its twin.

"What would you like to drink?" he asked.

"I'll have a citrus green tea on ice," Delva answered.

Nodding, he made his way to the counter. She watched his tall, muscular frame with appreciative eyes. Even though she knew he had to be at least five years older than her, he was very attractive.

His return with their drinks broke her reverie. He sat across from her, sliding her drink across the table. "I should have asked if you wanted sugar."

Delva smiled. "No, it's fine. I take my tea unsweetened."

He sipped from the small mug of coffee he bought for himself. Silence reigned between them for a moment. Then, out of the blue, he asked, "What color are your eyes?"

Puzzled, she raised a hand to her brow. "What?"

"You're wearing contacts." It was a statement, not a question. "I want to know you, the real you. So what color are they?"

His gaze was so intense, Delva shivered. No man had ever asked her such a probing question. It meant Alan Rupert was actually spending time looking into her eyes, not at her makeup, or her clothes, or down her dress.

It was different... but refreshing.

So, she turned away from him for a moment, and removed the Kelly green contacts. Fishing in her purse, she put them away in the container she kept there. When she raised her eyes back to Alan's, they were their natural color.

He smiled. "So I was right. They're caramel, like aged brandy." He reached across the table, capturing her hand in his. "And they are absolutely beautiful. Don't ever hide them behind those contacts again."

Delva could feel the heat filling her cheeks. His sultry voice and kind words touched her to the core. As much as she wanted to, she couldn't look away from him.

He got up, making a slow move around to her side of the table. She looked up at him, wonder washing over her.

Cupping her face in his gentle hands, he leaned down and kissed her. His warm lips crushed hers, and she trembled. Her eyes slid closed. The kiss deepened, and she allowed him to dip his tongue between her parted lips.

When he pulled away, she shimmered inside like sunlight on the surface of the ocean. He was one hell of a man, and his very presence overwhelmed her.

She opened her eyes and found him watching her. Sliding over, she patted the cushion. He slid onto the bench next to her.

"No man has ever paid enough attention to my eyes to care about the color before." Delva reached out with a trembling hand, stroking his cheek.

He kissed her forehead. "I'm not like any other man. I'm older, wiser. I know a quality woman when I see one, no matter how young or insecure she may be." His knowing eyes burned into hers. "I'm not after your body, darling. I'm after your heart."

His words were like a caress. She allowed herself to in his embrace. "You may have already won it."

*

Bright and early the next morning, the courthouse bustled with reporters and photographers. All the local news stations were there for the sentencing; the shooting at the ritzy country club generated a great deal of public interest.

Pope sat in the hot seat once again, next to his lawyer, staring into the disapproving face of Judge Carter.

"Mr. Pope," Judge Carter began, once court was called to order. "I have read your file with great interest. Let me just say that you have a pattern of violence against Mrs. Holdron and her family I find disturbing." She leaned forward. "Mr. Pope, I have considered the evidence presented to me, and I am sentencing you to thirty years in the Florida State Men's Correctional Facility. Also, because this state abolished parole in nineteen ninety-eight, you will serve your full sentence. I suggest you use the time to better yourself. That is my ruling." She banged her gavel.

As the correctional officer came to escort him away, he looked at Skye for what would likely be the last time. When she noticed him staring, he called to her.

"I'm sorry -- for everything." His heart heavy, Maurice Pope turned away from Skye as he was led to his fate.

He knew it wasn't over. Soon, his lawyer would be back in court, facing the civil case Skye and Kyoko brought against him. It seemed his past deeds had caught up with him, and ruined his life. Now, he'd be bringing in the New Year at the Florida State Prison.

Chapter 20
January 2006

"Oh!"

Kyoko was jolted from her sleep by the pain gripping her lower abdomen. Glancing at the digital clock on the nightstand, she noted the time: 1:36 AM.

Just as she tried to close her eyes, the pain returned.

"Jasper!" She jabbed the loudly snoring form next to her with her elbow. "Wake up!"

"What...what's the matter?" he asked sleepily.

"Ugh!" Kyoko grunted, as yet another pain gripped her. "We're having a baby, idiot!" Her tone held all the frustration she felt from the pain.

"We gotta go to the hospital!" Jasper jumped out of bed and grabbed a pair of jeans slung over the chair near the bed.

"Yeah, genius, how'd you come to that conclusion?" Kyoko gritted her teeth as he helped her stand up and get into her bathrobe and slippers.

Jasper held her shoulders, turning her to face him. "You are about to give me the best gift a woman can give a man. I know you're in pain, so yell at me all you want. It's not going to affect my gratitude."

Touched by his words, Kyoko smiled briefly. But as the baby began to somersault inside her, she pushed him. "Put your shoes on. Where's my bag?"

Jasper slid his feet into his black corduroy house shoes and dashed to the closet, returning with the bag they packed weeks ago. It contained clothes and toiletries for Kyoko and the baby. "I've got it."

Slinging the bag's strap over his shoulder, he swept his

petite wife into his arms. His back didn't enjoy the extra weight of the baby as he carried her downstairs as fast as he could without falling. Kyoko grabbed the keys off the hook next to the front door, and Jasper allowed her to lock the door behind them before walking to their recently purchased family SUV as fast as he could.

Arriving at the hospital in less than ten minutes, Jasper helped Kyoko out of the car and fetched the bag. He escorted her to a wheelchair parked near the south entrance.

"May I help you?" the receptionist asked, peering over her gold-rimmed glasses as Jasper wheeled Kyoko to the desk. Even though it was obvious what was going on, she had to ask.

"My wife is in labor," Jasper huffed. "We've already pre-registered."

"Take her up to labor and delivery on the fifth floor. I'll call ahead so they'll know you're coming." She pointed to the nearby elevator bank.

"Thank you!" Jasper shouted over his shoulder, as he pushed Kyoko to the first elevator.

A few minutes later, he wheeled the now howling Kyoko into labor and delivery. A friendly looking nurse clad in blue scrubs greeted him. "Mr. and Mrs. Holdron?"

"Yes," Kyoko answered between screams. "Baby's coming..."

"We'd better get her into a suite right away," the nurse commented, as she took over pushing the chair. "Looks like she's right in the thick of it. I'm Kate, by the way."

A worried Jasper followed Kate and the speeding wheelchair down the corridor, until she arrived in the room. Kate helped Kyoko onto the bed that was the centerpiece of the room, then helped her get out of her robe and panties. "Try to get comfortable," she told Kyoko, stroking her sweaty brow. "I'll be back ASAP with the doctor, okay?"

Before she could dash out, Kyoko grabbed her hand. "Bring...painkillers!"

After Kate left, Jasper went to his wife's side, clutching her hand. He watched her face contort in agony, realizing he'd never felt so helpless in his whole life. "I love you, Ky." It was all he could say.

"I...love you...too..." Kyoko's tears were running freely now, from a combination of pain and emotion.

Soon, Dr. Johnson entered the suite. "Good Job, Mrs. Holdron, your baby chose to be born on a night I was doing rounds!"

Kyoko smiled slightly, happy to see her familiar and friendly face. "Help, Doc...baby's coming..."

Dr. Johnson washed her hands and pulled on a pair of latex gloves. Kate assisted her into a green overcoat, which she put on over her chest to protect her scrubs, and a plastic face shield. "Let's have a look." She approached the bed and took a seat on the stool at the foot of it. Kate assisted Kyoko with putting her legs into the stirrups as Jasper looked on anxiously.

Once Dr. Johnson got a good look between Kyoko's legs, her eyes widened. "Whoa! You're nine and a half centimeters dilated, Mrs. Holdron. And the baby is already crowning." She gestured to Kate, who produced some mineral oil from a nearby supply cart. "I'm afraid it's a little late for pain meds. I'm going to perform a perineum massage, Mrs. Holdron. This will hopefully keep you from tearing, because this little one isn't going to wait for that last half centimeter."

Blowing out hard, Kyoko nodded. "Just...get it out... please."

"Kate, get neonatology in here, will you, hon?" Dr. Johnson worked furiously to help the baby move easily through the canal. She briefly glanced at Jasper, who was still clutching Kyoko's hand, but watching her work. "You're going to be a daddy very soon, Mr. Holdron."

Jasper nodded, then shifted his focus back to his wife. He still wished to take away the pain, but he knew it would be over soon.

The neonatologist Kate paged soon entered the room. "Hi, I'm Dr. Paltridge. I'll be taking a look at your baby to make sure she's healthy." He addressed Jasper, but he was focused on the birth of his daughter, he only nodded.

"Kate, I need those chucks..." Dr. Johnson worked to free the baby's shoulders from the birth canal. As soon as the nurse came with the stack of disposable hospital pads, Jasper watched in awe as his daughter slid out, pink, slippery and crying vigorously.

"Oh my God..." Kyoko breathed out, as Dr. Johnson laid her on her mother's abdomen. "She's so beautiful."

Jasper didn't realize he was crying until a teardrop splashed onto the white hospital sheet covering his wife. He looked on in absolute amazement as they toweled off the squirming bundle, and placed a pink hat on her tiny head. When they whisked the baby to Dr. Paltridge for her newborn screening, Jasper's wet, glistening eyes turned to Kyoko, who was looking across the room at their child.

"Ky..." he began, stroking her damp face. "Thank you."

Kyoko smiled sweetly up at him. "No sweat." She paused, addressing Kate. "I'm gonna need that pain medicine, please."

As the screening neared completion, Dr. Johnson presented the freshly scrubbed and bundled baby girl to Jasper. "I think someone would like to meet you, Mr. Holdron."

Jasper took the tiny, precious child into his arms, and was so overwhelmed with love that he thought his heart might burst. "Hi, sweetheart. I'm your daddy."

Those little eyes opened, and Jasper found himself

looking into two brown pools that had obviously been inherited from Kyoko.

"What's her name?" Kate asked Kyoko, as they looked on.

"Mitsuki. It means 'bright child'. And Nancy, after her grandmother."

In those little brown eyes, Jasper saw his whole future. And he looked forward to what it held for him and his new family.

*

When the nineteenth arrived, Maurice had been transported to the Florida State Prison to serve out his sentence, and wouldn't be present for the proceedings. However, in a rear corner of the room sat Nathan Pope, dressed in black, and keeping a low profile. His dark glasses and fedora obscured his identity from the prying eyes around him.

As Skye sat next to Alan Rupert, Harold Howe and Kyoko at the plaintiff's table, she turned around, her eyes scanning the courtroom. Her parents and Delva sat three rows back. There were many familiar faces in the crowd, and to her surprise, she saw her old boss, David Fitzpatrick, sitting in the back row. Their eyes met, and he waved. Waving back, Skye turned to Lawrence, who was sitting with Jasper and the baby, directly behind her on the first row.

"I saw him," Lawrence said, as she gestured toward the back. "It was very nice of him to come."

Skye's attention was called to the front as the bailiff announced that court was in session. Everyone present stood as the judge entered.

Judge Reginald Pettiford took his seat behind the bench. His tall, wide frame and serious demeanor demanded respect, and as he straightened his tie and banged his gavel, Cheniqua Gray tried to hide her nervousness. Judge Pettiford had a reputation for being tough on violent defendants, especially those who chose women as their victims.

"Please be seated," Judge Pettiford began. "This is civil case one-one-zero-nine-eight, Skye Lynne Donovan Holdron and Kyoko Mai Yamanaka-Holdron versus Maurice Gregory Pope." He shuffled through a stack of papers in front of him, then looked toward Cheniqua. "I understand Mr. Pope couldn't be present today, as he had a previous engagement with Warden Hall at the Florida State Prison." His wry smile reflected the humor in his statement. "Counsel Gray, I assume you have Mr. Pope's answer?"

"Yes, your honor." Cheniqua stood. "My client admitted to the allegations brought against him, and he's asked that I not contest Mr. Rupert and Mr. Howe on what their clients are seeking. I have his written statement here." She approached the bench and handed a piece of paper to the judge.

After taking several moments to read the letter, Judge Pettiford spoke, this time to Alan Rupert. "It would appear Mr. Pope is remorseful for his crimes. He hopes agreeing to your demands will help ease your clients' pain." He paused. "Therefore, I am ordering the sale of all Mr. Pope's real property, including his practice and two homes. And I am awarding your clients six hundred fifty thousand dollars each to cover medical bills, pain and suffering..."

Suddenly, the judge was cut off by an impassioned shout from the back of the room. "I object to that!"

Judge Pettiford searched the room until he found the source of the interruption, a middle-aged man wearing all black. "Excuse me, sir, but I'm in the middle of a ruling.

And let me give you a glimpse into 'Courtroom One-oh-One'. Only the lawyers can make objections."

The man scoffed, removing his hat and sunglasses to reveal his angry face. "You'll not sell that practice. I paid for it! This is outrageous!"

Judge Pettiford stood, visibly irritated. "Now, sir, I'll have to ask you to sit down and shut up, before I have the bailiff drag your self righteous, pretentious carcass out of my courtroom!" He waited for the rude man to take his seat, and then sat down, clearing his throat. "As I was saying, both Mrs. Holdrons will receive six hundred fifty thousand dollars each. That is my ruling."

The man started to stand, but before he could speak, Judge Pettiford saw him. "Sir, would you like to be held in contempt of court?"

Disgusted and pouting like a spoiled child, he stalked out of the courtroom.

Judge Pettiford, satisfied, banged his gavel. "I'll take the next case now."

*

Skye and Kyoko hugged each other tightly, squealing with delight. Jasper approached, handing his squirming daughter to her mother.

"Wow. I didn't think he'd just give us what we asked for," Kyoko said, smiling. "He owes it to us, though." She rubbed Mitsuki's tiny back, and she burped into her mother's shoulder in response. "Now the baby can go to college wherever she wants."

"Hey, I'm looking to get with a rich woman," Jasper said jokingly, wrapping his arms around Kyoko's waist. "Will you be my Sugar Mama?"

Kyoko and Skye both burst into giggles at Jasper's silliness. It was the first time in a while Kyoko had a hearty laugh, and it felt good.

As Jasper took Kyoko to shop for more baby clothes for their already spoiled and well-dressed child, Lawrence and Skye stopped so he could shake hands with his colleagues. "Thank you," he said sincerely, to both Alan and Harold.

"Don't mention it." Harold smiled. "We know you'd do the same for us."

Outside, Lawrence and Skye got into his truck. "So, where would you like to go, honey?"

Skye sighed, unable to hide her happiness. "Let's go to that bed and breakfast up in Palm Beach. You know, the one where we stayed on our fifth anniversary?"

"Sounds like a plan." Lawrence started the truck, and whisked his wife away to their own private paradise, where he planned to make her forget every hurt she'd suffered.

*

When they arrived at Pleasant Palms Bed and Breakfast, Lawrence escorted Skye into the lobby. At the front desk, he arranged for them to spend the next three nights there. When they received their room keys, he sent Skye upstairs to wait for him while he retrieved their luggage from the car.

Soon, they were lying together in the king-sized bed, atop a down feather-bed and luxurious sateen sheets.

"Wow," Lawrence mumbled as he squeezed Skye. "I can't believe what a year this had been."

"Tell me about it," Skye sighed as she sank into the feather-bed. "But you know what they say. If it doesn't kill you, it only makes you stronger." She smiled at her husband of eleven years, then kissed him deeply. "I love you, Lawrence. I don't know what I would have done without you."

He grinned. "I love you, too. But you didn't need me. You always had the inner strength to do whatever you set your mind to, including whipping Pope's ass. You just didn't know it."

One by one, Lawrence pulled the bobby pins from his wife's up swept hair, until it fell on the pillow, framing her beautiful face like a glossy, coffee-colored halo. Pulling her close again, he kissed her passionately. His hands roamed her body, seeking to awaken parts of her that had been neglected during the stressful times of the past few weeks. She sighed as he tugged at her dress, pulling it away from her body. Lifting her hips, he dragged her white satin panties down.

Skye lay half dressed and fully aroused before him. Lawrence marveled at her lush beauty as his erection demanded release from his boxers.

He stood, quickly stripping off his business suit and undergarments. As he returned to her, she surprised him by sitting up and filling her hand with his aching hardness. When she guided it into her mouth, he felt he would explode. Somehow, he managed to hold back as her hot little mouth threatened to draw his very soul out. Skye moaned around the thick hardness and he began to squirm. Before he could do anything, Skye quickly moved up, sinking down onto his iron hardness. They both sighed with abandon as two became one.

Lawrence's eyes closed briefly as he penetrated her then opened. He watched the subtle bounce of her breasts, glistening with a sheen of perspiration as she gyrated above him, her midsection undulating like that of a belly dancer. He held her shapely hips, filling his hands as she rode him. When she began to shiver above him, he knew she was close. Quickly, he overtook her, turning her over on her back and pressing deep into her. He held her legs up, the backs of her knees resting in the crooks of his elbows, as he pounded away. Moments later, orgasm swept him away.

Laying on her chest, he breathed out. "Sorry, it's been

awhile."

Her answering chuckle was the last sound he heard before he fell asleep.

*

Later that week, Skye went with Cammie to the bridal shop for her final fitting. They were joined at the shop by Cammie's mother, Elizabeth, and the three other women Cammie chose to stand with her on the most important day of her life.

Cammie's gown was a strapless, satin and chiffon Vera Wang design. The fitted bodice was encrusted with pearls and rhinestones, and the full skirt fell gracefully to the floor, ending in a chapel-length train, accented by more tiny pearls and stones. As she stood in front of the mirror, wearing the tiara Skye had given her, Cammie smiled at the woman reflected there.

"Cammie," Skye said. "You look beautiful. You're going to take Wayne's breath away." She dabbed at her eyes, wondering why she was so emotional.

"That's my plan." Cammie stepped down from the platform. "I think Mom agrees with you." She gestured to Elizabeth, who sat nearby, sobbing into her linen handkerchief.

"Oh, my darling baby," Elizabeth said, between sobs. "You look more beautiful than I've ever seen you." Her exaggerated Southern drawl was a product of her Memphis upbringing and Charleston residence. "I'm so happy I could do a little jig!"

"Please don't, Mom," Cammie said, with a giggle. "At least not in public."

After Cammie took off the dress and had it wrapped, she and Skye went over to Bellini's for a quiet dinner.

"I'm so happy for you, Cammie. Nobody deserves this

more than you," Skye said, as she lifted a forkful of seafood linguine to her lips.

"Well," Cammie began, sipping from a chilled glass of chardonnay, "I couldn't have gotten everything together without you. You're more like a sister to me than a best friend."

"For a while, you were more like a sister to me than my blood sister." Skye gazed out the window. "I really love you, girl."

"I love you, too, Skye. You'll always be my partner in crime." The two friends shared a hug over their plates.

When they finished their meal, they parted ways as the sun set over Boca Raton, painting the sky with blues, oranges and purples as it descended.

Chapter 21
February 2006

Skye's parents arrived late January to spend a week with her and Lawrence. Delva joined them, and even though she spent most of her time in town with Alan Rupert, she made sure to be there for Sunday dinner.

Skye and Mary laid out quite a spread, and there was plenty of honey-cured ham, roasted turkey, dressing, yams, potato salad, and collard greens to go around. After dinner, they gathered around the fireplace and enjoyed some homemade sweet potato pie while Louis told embarrassing stories about Skye and Delva's childhood shenanigans.

The group sat and chatted. Alan approached Louis. "Mr. Donovan," he said, barely above a whisper, "could I speak with you for a moment?"

"Sure," Louis answered, and he and Alan went into the kitchen to talk. Once they sat down on the stools near the center island, he noticed Alan's serious expression. "What can I do for you?"

"Well, Mr. Donovan..."

"Aw, you can stop all that 'Mr. Donovan' stuff. Call me Louis."

"Yes, sir. Louis, I've been dating Delva for quite a few months now, and she is very special to me. I've fallen in love with your daughter."

Louis scratched his chin thoughtfully. "Are you asking what I think you're asking?"

Alan nodded. "Yes, sir. I'd like to make Delva my wife."

Louis stuck out his hand. "You've got my blessing, young man. I like you, and I think you'll be good for her."

Smiling, Alan shook hands with his future father-in-law. "Thank you, sir. I promise that Delva will never want for anything."

"Now that's what a father likes to hear." Louis chuckled, standing.

As the two men walked back into the living room, Mary Jean eyed her husband curiously. "What was that all about?" she probed when he sat down next to her.

"Soon, all will be revealed," was all Louis said.

*

Alan went immediately to Delva's side. Once there, he called out, "May I have everyone's attention, please?"

All eyes in the room fell on Alan, especially those of a very concerned Mary Jean.

"I want you all to bear witness to this," Alan dropped to one knee before Delva, who immediately placed a hand over her mouth. "Maybe, with your whole family watching us, you won't be able to turn me down when I ask you to be my wife."

Delva's eyes glistened with tears as Alan produced a small black box from his coat pocket. Opening it, he revealed a stunning, three carat, princess cut diamond on a platinum band. "Delva, I love you more than anything this life has to offer. Will you marry me?"

Still clutching her mouth Delva nodded, tears flowing down her cheeks.

The room erupted into applause and well wishes as Delva stood and laid a kiss on Alan that threatened to straighten his hair.

On the sofa, Mary Jean wept openly, overjoyed at this surprising turn of events. "My baby...getting...married..." she shouted out between sobs.

Skye and Lawrence smiled knowingly at each other. He

reached for Skye's hand and kissed it. "You know what the Good Book says, baby," he whispered, his eyes on Delva and Alan. "He who findeth a wife," he paused, his eyes landing on his own beautiful bride, "findeth a good thing."

Skye winked at him and kissed him on the cheek. "You know it."

That night, after their guests had gone, Skye and Lawrence bundled up in their winter coats and scarves to enjoy some quiet time on the patio.

"Wow. Delva's getting married," Lawrence stated, as if trying to get used to the idea. "I just can't see her cooking and cleaning and being...wife-like."

"Well, she doesn't know how to do that stuff," Skye said, sipping from a mug of hot chocolate. "But for a man as fine as Alan, I'm sure she'll learn." She giggled at the thought of Delva, wearing an apron and attempting to cook. "Let's just pray she doesn't burn the house down."

Skye moved from her seat and sat down on Lawrence's lap, and they enjoyed the clear, starry night together.

*

New Year's Day dawned bright and crisp. Cammie stood near the window of the presidential suite of the Brampton Inn, a steaming mug of coffee in hand, as the sun peeked over the horizon. Her hair in a mass of multicolored curlers, she gazed out at the city below her, dreaming of the day held in store.

"Good morning," a soft, female voice called behind her.

Cammie turned and Skye stood there. Her friend's hair was wrapped in a print silk scarf, and she wore a pair of mint green silk pajamas.

"Cammie, why are you up so early?"

She pulled her cotton hotel robe tighter around her body. "I couldn't sleep. I was too excited."

Skye shook her head, smiling. "It's kind of like being a kid on Christmas Eve again, isn't it? I remember that feeling very well."

Cammie nodded. "That's a pretty accurate description." She plopped down in the ivory armchair in the center of the room. "Do you think we should get everyone together for breakfast? It's seven-thirty," she remarked, glancing at the wall clock.

"Hey, why not? It's your day. I'm sure they won't mind getting up a little early."

Crossing the sitting area and entering the short hallway, she first roused Tara, Cammie's maid of honor, from the double bed she snored in. Skye made her way to the front of the suite, and knocked on the door of the adjoining room. A groggy, nightgown-clad Sarah, Cammie's cousin, slid the door open.

"What is it?" Sarah stifled a yawn.

"Wake up Lora and Val. We're about to get breakfast."

Sarah rubbed her eyes. "What time is it?"

"About seven-forty. Cammie's up with the sun today. Just come over when you get ready."

Sarah nodded, closing the door. Skye glided back into the sitting room, where Cammie twiddled her thumbs. "I'll get on the phone with room service, and have the deluxe continental breakfast delivered to us. Trust me, you don't want a heavy breakfast. Wedding day nerves can make your stomach turn against you."

Within half an hour, Cammie and her attendants enjoyed a lovely breakfast of assorted pastries, fresh fruit and orange juice. Skye stood, raising her juice glass high.

"To Cammie. May this be the most kick-ass day of her life!"

The small group of women erupted into cheers and applause. After finishing their food, they rode over to the church to prepare the blushing bride for her walk down the aisle.

*

Cammie and her father, Frank, waited in the vestibule of the big church.

"You look stunning," Frank told his daughter, as he linked arms with her.

"Thanks, Dad." Cammie did her best to hold her tears at bay.

When the ceremony started moments later, the processional moved slowly down the aisle. As the doors opened and Cammie stepped in, her eyes fell on Wayne. He stood at the altar, tapping his foot and looking decidedly nervous. She offered him a watery smile, which he returned. When she stood next to him, he took her gloved hand, and they turned to face the pastor.

The ceremony was heartwarming. Wayne and Cammie looked deeply into each others' eyes as they said their vows. They held hands as they lit the unity candle.

"I now pronounce you man and wife," the pastor proclaimed. Cammie jumped up and down, unable to contain her excitement. "You may now kiss the bride."

Wayne grabbed her, dipping her low as they kissed. Hoots and cheers rose from the onlookers.

The smiling reverend announced, "I now introduce to you all -- Mr. and Mrs. Wayne O'Leary." They walked out of the church to the thunderous applause of their guests, and entered the waiting limo surrounded by a shower of bubbles.

*

In the grand ballroom of the Renaissance Boca Raton, the reception was held. The twinkling glow of white lights strung from the ceiling and candles in the white gardenia centerpieces filled the room with a romantic glow. The guests mingled and danced to the hits of the eighties, and feasted on the sumptuous buffet the hotel chef and his staff prepared. As Edward Norton, the best man, tapped his glass with a fork, the guests settled down, and all eyes turned toward the head table.

"I've known these two lovebirds their whole relationship," he began, "and I've known Wayne most of his life. I never thought he'd get married. He was always a playboy; love 'em and leave 'em in need of therapy!" Edward smiled, pausing as the crowd erupted into laughter. "But, seriously folks, when he met Camilla, something changed about him. He has become a better person, just by virtue of having her in his life." He raised his glass, and the guests followed suit. "So, to the bride and groom, many years of joy, fruitfulness, and good old sanity."

Just after the couple's first dance, to Whitesnake's "Is This Love," Skye and Lawrence decided to hit the floor for a dance of their own. She glanced around and noticed Alan and Delva, dancing cheek to cheek.

"Look at Delva and Alan. They've been attached at the hip for weeks now." Lawrence shook his head.

Skye smiled knowingly. "Delva says Alan accepts her the way she is. She's given up those crazy hats. I'm glad they found each other. I want my sister to be happy."

Steps away from Delva and Alan were Kyoko and Jasper. He twirled her around, and she laughed at something he whispered in her ear. Skye knew from talking to Kyoko earlier that 'Grandpa Teddy' was watching the baby.

The band ended its set, and left the stage for a break. Skye clapped and cheered when she was overcome by a wave of nausea. Covering her mouth with her hand, she rushed into the nearest restroom.

When she returned, she was greeted by a concerned Lawrence. "Are you okay?"

"I don't feel so hot," Skye sipped from her water glass. "I must have eaten too much." She placed a hand on her rumbling stomach.

"Do you want to go home?"

"No, no...I just need to sit down for a minute."

Lawrence pulled out Skye's chair so she could sit. She managed to sit through most of the reception, but around the night wore on, she could no longer stand it.

"Okay," Skye relented. "I need to go home now." She spotted Cammie in the crowd, and trudged over to her. "Cammie, I've got to go. I feel really sick. I'm sorry I can't stay longer..."

Cammie hugged her best friend. "It's okay. Wayne and I are leaving soon, anyway. Go home and get yourself some rest, okay?" She gave Skye a kiss on the cheek, and Lawrence escorted her outside.

Before they could make it, however, Skye made a detour to the bushes next to the hotel so she could throw up again.

"That's it," Lawrence said, as he handed her his handkerchief. "I'm taking you to the emergency room."

Skye lay in a hospital bed in the emergency department of Boca Raton Community Hospital, looking positively green. She had a battery of tests performed, and between all the blood drawn, the urine sample, and the continuous vomiting, she felt as if there weren't a drop of liquid left in her body. Skye wrinkled her nose as she sipped from a paper cup of cold water, displeased with the antiseptic smells that surrounded her.

Lawrence sat in a chair nearby, watching over his wife while he waited for the doctor to return with her test results.

"Hi, I'm Dr. Monroe. I understand you're feeling pretty bad." He paused as he flipped through the pages on his clipboard. "I have your test results here, and there's a perfectly good reason why you feel so awful."

"Is it food poisoning?" Skye asked, worried.

"No, ma'am. You're about sixteen weeks pregnant."

"What? Are you sure?" Lawrence stood, unable to hide his excitement.

"Yes, sir. The blood test is ninety-nine point nine percent accurate." Dr. Monroe pulled a pad from his lab coat pocket. "I'll write a prescription for some anti-nausea medication. That should help you keep your food down." He scribbled it down, handing it to Lawrence. "See that your wife gets plenty of rest and fluids, and she should be fine."

Lawrence took the paper, heartily shaking his hand. "Thank you, Doctor."

Once the doctor left the room, Lawrence helped Skye to stand and pulled her into his arms. "Oh, baby. I'm gonna take such good care of you."

Skye smiled, tears of joy streaming down her face. "I know, Lawrence. You always have."

The End

Author's Note

I first began work on this book, initially titled <u>Skye's the Limit</u>, in 2004. At the time, I knew next to nothing about the business of writing. I had a good command of grammar, sentence structure; the nuts and bolts of writing. But the business side was a mystery to me. As much as I love to read, one would think I'd come into this writing thing with more knowledge of what it would be like. I had no idea just how complex the publishing industry could be.

I'm a lifelong reader, and I've had a love affair with words since an early age. Books have always been my favorite escape, to this day I prefer them over television, or any other entertainment media. It wasn't until I reached prepubescence that I started journaling my thoughts and jotting down the stories that seemed to pop into my head at random intervals. I was about eleven when I wrote my first play, "The Dream," based on a dream I'd had. It would be more than a decade before I made the transition from being a reader to thinking of myself as a writer.

Once I began think of writing a serious pursuit, and started to study the industry, I discovered a lot of information. I found that my perception of the publishing industry as a reader were vastly different from the reality writers face. As a reader, I assumed writers were respected and venerated, regardless of genre; I assumed they were paid well and made a great living at writing the stories that entertain and inform us; I assumed everyone a writer encountered would be courteous and professional. Instead, I discovered that writing is looked down upon by many people, who don't even consider it a "real job." Even within the industry, writers of certain "serious" genres look down on writers of genres they consider to have less merit. As far as money, for writers, there are no guarantees. Even with a great book, a writer might make little to no money. And within the industry, there are people who are supposed to be professionals, but are actually rude, dishonest, and downright unscrupulous. It was a lot to take in. Still, the dream of writing was so strong within me that I chose to pursue it despite all the pitfalls I would likely encounter.

The process of writing this book was a long, tedious one. I had to learn genre conventions, so I would know how to write a story that fit into an accepted category. I had to learn how to "show" the events of the story, rather than "tell" them. I had to embrace the story that was inside of me, and try to stay true to it, while making it salable. I was learning as I went along, writing when I had free time, hoping to someday have a completed manuscript.

During the initial writing, I was staying at the home of an older cousin, Tonya. (Yes, the one mentioned in the dedication.) I was living with her for a short period of time to be near to my new husband, who was having health difficulties at the time, and was training at a military base near her home. My cousin was a good twelve years my senior, and was a working woman with two children in high school. That meant most days, for the three months I lived there, I was home alone all day with the dog. It was during those long days that I decided to sit down at Tonya's computer and begin writing.

One day, Tonya returned home from work, and asked what I was working on. My answer was pretty non-committal. "Um, it's a story. Maybe a book...I don't really know yet." She immediately asked to see it, and I printed out the first two chapters, which was all I'd written. I stayed in the office while she went to her room to read it, amazed that anyone would be interested in what I'd written.

When she emerged, she had a look on her face that even I have a hard time describing. Let's call it amazement. She said, "You have to finish this book. I want you to write a chapter a day, and I'll read what you write when I come home."

Wide-eyed, I said, "I don't know if I will finish."

Tonya disagreed. "Yes, you will. If you don't have a chapter when I come home, you won't eat in this house."

That got me to agree. And Tonya was serious, because she locked the deep freezer every morning, and took the key with her to work. Besides, she didn't try to keep me out of the fridge, the idea was to get me to write, not to starve me. I still ate, just nothing particularly substantial until I'd turned in my pages at the day's end. Day by day, chapter by chapter, I sat down and wrote. I didn't outline the book, so at times I had no idea where I was going, or what my characters would do next, but I just kept tapping away at the keys. It wasn't just about food (though I do enjoy eating,) it was about proving that I could finish a book, and making the best use of my time.

To some, her tactic might sound harsh, but it was just what I needed. I thank her to this very day for what she did, and that's why she's mentioned in the dedication. What Tonya did for me cannot be overstated. I was a very distant relative, she'd never met me before, and yet she took me into her home for several months, and gave me the time and resources to write. She never asked for compensation of any kind, all she asked was that I finish. Because of her, I was able to release the story trapped in my heart and in my head, and get it down on paper. Unfortunately, Tonya passed away suddenly in July of 2013, but I'm so glad I was able to communicate my gratitude to her while she was still here. I still credit that winter I spent at her house in Virginia for launching my writing career.

Once I returned home to North Carolina with my husband, I went about the business of being a wife. Tucking the manuscript away, I kept house, cooked meals, and did the shopping for me and my husband, who was still serving in the military. Consumed with setting up and running a household, I neglected my writing for a long time, a little over two years. During that time, my husband and I had our first child, a son, born with Down syndrome. Taking care of him became another full time job, but when he was a young infant, he was very quiet and sweet. He didn't demand very much, rarely cried, and seemed content just to be near me. With my baby swaddled and tucked into his little bouncy seat at my feet, I began to use that quiet time to revisit my writing.

I finished the third draft in 2007, then began the process of submitting it to publishers and agents, hoping someone would see my work as valuable and worthy enough for publication. In 2008, I attended my first Romance Slam Jam conference. That year it was held in Chicago, and I was lured there mainly by the knowledge that my writing idol, Beverly Jenkins, would be in attendance. I went there with my bags full of business attire, printed and labeled copies of my manuscript query letters, and a heart full of dreams. I pitched to two editors and one agent that year, and my enthusiasm was so high that all of them requested my manuscript. I got to spend a bit of time with Beverly as well, and that has proven to be one of the most significant relationships in my life, not just as it pertains to writing. These days, I consider Beverly a mentor, a close friend, a confidant, and a mother figure.

I submitted as requested to all the professionals who

asked for my book, and they all rejected it. Still, they also took time to write me detailed notes on how I might improve the book, so I spent the next several months doing just that. I edited, I rewrote, I slashed and burned, and rebuilt. Then I began sending out submissions again, and this time, I got an acceptance. I can clearly remember the joy I felt the day I got the call from the editor at the small press who published the book. My mother, husband, and son were all in the house with me. When I heard the news, I screamed, drawing my husband's attention. Ending the call, I shared the news with my family, and we all jumped up and down and acted quite silly for several minutes. My son, who was just around eighteen months old, sat on the floor and watched us all as if we'd gone crazy. Most writer's who've experienced "The Call" can tell you how exciting it is. It represents validation, something the fragile writer of an ego craves.

The book was first published in August of 2009. It's been a decade since I wrote the first sentence of the book, one of the few sentences that remained through all the edits and changes the manuscript has gone through. I now have nearly twenty books published, have parted on less than ideal terms with that first publisher, and have taken a chance on my work buy independently publishing it. When I first started out, I wanted validation from agents and publishers. Now that validation comes from those who are most vital to my writing career- my readers. I've traveled to conferences and book events all over the US, and met my readers face to face. Meeting them, and hearing them talk about my characters and the stories I've written in such glowing terms is my favorite part of being an author. I can't tell you what a fantastic group of people they are. My readers inspire me in ways I can't fathom. They are what keeps me from giving up when it becomes too hard to write another word.

When I decided to re-release the book, I first considered yet another slash and burn rewriting of the manuscript. Then, I decided against that. While it's true my writing has grown and evolved a lot since this book was published, I think there is value in preserving it the way I wrote it. I know readers may compare it to my later works, and I'm fine with that. But this will always be my first published book, and to me there is something a bit sacred about that. In honor of the tears I shed, the doubts I faced down, and all the labor I put into it, I decided to leave it as it is. After all, for people who've never read it before, the story will always be a new one.

I've learned so much in the last decade, and I've learned it in the trenches of the industry. I've seen publishers come and go. Larger companies seem to have a habit of absorbing smaller ones, and smaller houses flounder and go out of business all the time. I've met so many writers who've helped and inspired me, as well as met new writers who remind me of what it was like when I started in the business. I've also experienced first hand what it means to be an African American woman writing romance in a publishing industry that sometimes wants to marginalize what I write, or ignore it altogether. The industry is always changing, but for me, one thing has remained the same.

I am a writer. There's no changing it, it's part of who I am. Writing is what I'm meant to do, and I must do it. And if you keep reading, I'll keep writing.

For those who've been there since the beginning, thanks for taking the ride with me. And if you're new, welcome aboard.

All the Best,
Kianna

The Object of His Obsession

OTHER TITLES BY

Kianna Alexander

*denotes a title available in print

eBooks available at Amazon, B&N, iBooks, Kobo

Graham's Goddesses(Sensual Historical Romance)

from Ellora's Cave Publishing

Freedom's Embrace

Love's Lasso

Deputy's Desire

The Roses of Ridgeway (Sweet Historical Romance)

*Kissing the Captain

*The Preacher's Paramour

*Loving the Lawman

*Roses of Ridgeway, Volume 1 (Contains all 3 books)

Phoenix Files (Sensual Contemporary Paranormal Romance)

*Darkness Rising

*Embrace the Night

*Midnight's Serenade

*The Phoenix Files Trilogy (Contains all 3 books)

ABOUT

THE

Author

Kianna Alexander loves to regale readers with romantic tales that touch the heart. Kianna wears many hats: wife to her childhood sweetheart, mother to two very precocious youngsters, sister, advisor, friend, and purveyor of all things awesome. She lives in the mid-Atlantic US with her family. When not writing, she enjoys reading, listening to music, goofing off on social media, and playing hidden object games.

For more, visit the author's website:

www.AuthorKiannaAlexander.com

Find her on social media by searching "KiannaWrites" on Facebook, Twitter, and Pinterest

The Object of His Obsession

WANT *More?*

Scan the code to visit Kianna's website, sign up for her new release mailing list, and keep up with her appearances, contests, and more.

Kianna Alexander

FALL IN LOVE...BETWEEN THE PAGES OF A BOOK
www.AuthorKiannaAlexander.com

Made in the USA
Las Vegas, NV
24 January 2025